PRINTED AND PUBLISHED BY JAS. JAMES,
"CAXTON PRESS," CASTLE STREET, MAESTEG.

MAYSON AT THE AGE OF 65.

WALTER H. MAYSON:

An account of the Life and
Work of a Celebrated
Modern Violin Maker,

WITH NUMEROUS ILLUSTRATIONS,

BY THE

Rev. W. MEREDITH MORRIS, B.A.,

*F.R Hist. S.; Member of the Society
of Arts; Author of "British Violin
Makers: Classical and Modern," etc.*

PUBLISHED BY SUBSCRIPTION.

MAESTEG:
J. JAMES, "CAXTON PRESS," 12 CASTLE STREET.
1906.

CONTENTS.

———

═══════

APPENDICES.

———

PREFACE.

This little volume is an appreciation of the life and work of a good man and a great artist. It does not pretend to any merit as a biography, nor to daintiness as a literary morsel. As a biography it is fragmentary, and as literature it is commonplace. But it deals with two great verities, the good and the beautiful, and seeks to show how and in what proportion they meet and unite in the subject. The art of violin making never before received in Britain the attention that it does to-day, and a few words about one of its greatest exponents cannot fail to be of interest to those who dwell within the mystic circle of the Violin World.

THE AUTHOR.

GARTH PARSONAGE.

Chapter 1.

Birth and Childhood.

WALTER Henry Mayson was born at Cheetwood,
a quaint, straggling village situate about a
mile to the north of Manchester, on November 8,
1835. He was the fourth son of Mark and Elizabeth
Mayson, who had a family of eleven children—six
sons and five daughters. Mark Mayson was a descendant
of an ancient Cumberland family, and in the days
of his prosperity owned considerable property in
Keswick. Elizabeth Mayson's family name was Green,
she being a daughter of William and Ann Green,
of London, Manchester, and later of Ambleside.
William Green was the celebrated painter whose
excellent work is so highly esteemed by Professor
Wilson (Christopher North), Hartley, Coleridge, and
William Wordsworth. Wordsworth, it will be re-
membered, wrote the beautiful epitaph of Green with
which the reader is no doubt familiar:

"Sacred to the Memory of

William Green,

The last twenty-three years of whose life were
passed in this neighbourhood, where, by his skill

and industry as an artist, he produced faithful representations of the country, and lasting memorials of its more perishable fortunes. He was born at Manchester, and died at Ambleside on the 29th day of April, 1823, in the sixty-third year of his age, deeply lamented by a numerous family, and universally respected."

The mortal remains of both Wordsworth and Green lie in close proximity in the Grasmere churchyard. Christopher North used to boast that he had once carried Green on his back over a stream, and he was wont to say that England had produced only three painters, one of whom was William Green.

The words of the ancient law-giver bid us believe that the virtues of the wise descend unto their far-off posterity, and the language of modern science is not very dissimilar. It is not therefore contrary to expectation to find that a double portion of the grand-father's spirit had fallen on the budding "Stradivari," and that in mature life Mayson gave ample proof that he was made of the same material as the painter of Ambleside.

The house in which Walter Mayson first saw light of day is long since razed to the ground. Like many another old-world building of its kind, which sought peace too near the swelling tide of Cottonopolis' commerce, it has been swept the way of things transient. It was a small house for a large family, but

quite equal to the father's resources at the time of
Walter's youth. Mark Mayson was no longer the affluent
land owner of former years. He had lost his Keswick
estate through becoming security for a relative who had
sustained a heavy failure, and who had fled the country,
leaving his benefactor to face the burden and shame
of his disaster. Mark Mayson fell on evil days, and
was obliged to abandon the beautiful home at Keswick.
He went to Leeds, where he obtained employment as
clerk. Thence, after two years of toil and struggle,
he and the family removed again to Cheetwood,—he
obtaining employment as clerk in Manchester, where also
three of the sons found employment in various capacities.

The home at Cheetwood was poor, but not without
its blessings and comforts. Mrs. Mayson was an
accomplished woman and a wise mother, possessing in
an eminent degree the gift of adaptability, and she, at
least, accepted the change wrought by adverse circumstances with true christian resignation. She bore by
far the larger share of the increasing responsibility.
Her husband's despondency contrasted ill with her
dauntless courage and patient endurance. To help swell
the scanty earnings of her husband, whose wage was
never above twenty-five shillings a week, she opened
a small private school, teaching, in addition to the usual
subjects, French, Italian, music, and painting. Of his
mother's struggles, and of her affectionate regard for
the well-being of her family, Mayson retained the
tenderest recollections. He writes: "Why hide a pain
that reveals such a woman—the best my heart has ever

BIRTHPLACE OF MAYSON.

known? She was all in all to our home—a poor home, yet the abode of true affection. She would spend the day with her pupils, and the night in mending our clothes. Her happiest moment was when she succeeded, though but for a momemt, in lifting the veil of my father's melancholy, and when she watched her children play in guileless youth, unconscious of their parents' struggles."

One trivial incident belonging to this period of Mayson's life must be related here. It has been said that coming events cast their shadows before them : in that light the following childish event may be considered prophetic. One morning Walter found a half-penny, which he jubilantly showed his mother, who warned him not to tell a certain naughty lad with whom he used to play against her will. Needless to say, young Walter disregarded the warning, lost the half-penny, and received a sound drubbing for trying to defend his own. The incident made a lasting impression on the mind of the child, and the vicissitudes of after life served rather to deepen it than otherwise. Mayson was wont to say that, in the more serious game of life, he always came out "second best" in the art of defending his own.

After only a few years' residence the home in Cheetwood had to be broken up, and the family made another move to Cheetham Hill, a village situate nearly two miles further from Manchester, on the high road from Cheetwood. Here all the days of Mayson's boyhood and early manhood were spent. They were

mostly days of uneventful monotony, broken only
occasionally by some chance village exploit, or by the
periodical visit of a peripatetic Punch and Judy show.
Mrs. Mayson, in conjunction with two of her sisters,
opened a small school in the village, which proved so
successful that the prospects of the family brightened
considerably, and home comforts assumed the proportions
of luxury, as compared with the penury of recent years.
The elder sons, by their perseverance and good conduct,
had gradually worked their way up. Mark had
become cashier at a colliery in Dukinfield, Wilfred
was a captain of a small trading vessel, William
a designer to a firm of calico printers, and Martin
an apprentice at a warehouse in Manchester. Walter,
our subject, was sent to the celebrated school of
Thomas Whalley, and the sisters to a boarding school,
which was kept by two of their aunts, sisters to their
father, in the village.

Under the tuition of Whalley, Walter made rapid
progress. He distinguished himself more especially at
English composition, his essays being invariably selected
by the master for public reading before the school.
Their excellence elicited a deal of praise from the
master, and many hard blows from the pupils. One
day a big burly boy threw him down on the pave-
ment, and he was carried home with a deep gash on
the head, bleeding and fainting. Nevertheless he
continued to write excellent essays, and to advance
in his studies, so that before long he was the
acknowledged senior scholar of the school. Only two

further events punctuate the period of boyhood.
At the age of twelve Walter experienced one sharp
proof of his mother's inflexible probity—an experience
which had a lasting influence for good on his mind.
One day he was sent on an errand, when he cheated
his mother of a half-penny in the change. His
blushes and hesitation betrayed his guilt. With solemn
voice and eyes bedimmed with tears the good woman
rebuked the erring boy, compelling him to fall on
his knees to beg God's forgiveness. She prayed so
earnestly that God would have mercy on her child,
and lead him in the paths of righteousness, that the
lad's heart was so touched that he never again
attempted to cheat, or do aught else to grieve his
mother. The other event had far-reaching results,
awaking as it did within the boy's breast the dormant
impulses of his artistic nature. One fine morning
Mrs. Salis Schwabbe, the wife of an opulent merchant
of Manchester, who often called on Mrs. Mayson, brought
the immortal Jenny Lind to Cheetham Hill. The
prima donna presented the family with two reserved
tickets, one of which she put in the hands of young
Walter, whom she patted familiarly on the head and
questioned about his school lessons. To his inexpressible
delight Walter was permitted to accompany his mother
that evening to Manchester to hear the "Queen of
Song" in the "Elijah"—a glorious treat, which he
could not forget to his dying day.

MAYSON AT 19.

Chapter 2.

Manhood and Sorrow.

THE lad was now far up his teens, but he had shown as yet little or no indication of the course he was to follow in the future. Only he was a rare hand at making all sorts of bric-à-brac, and an adept at constructing ingenious fireworks. His restless ingenuity nearly cost him his life on one occasion. He had put some combustibles in a box on a shelf in the kitchen, and as he sat reading by the fire he heard an ominous fizzing. He seized the box and rushed with it to the garden, when, no sooner than he had dropped it at a safe distance from the house and taken shelter, it exploded with a loud report, scattering splinters of wood and glass in every direction. Mr. Mayson used to relate this little adventure with a merry twinkle, and he would add, " It might have been courage to rush at the box of combustibles, 1 know not, but I often think it was much on a par with my taking the terrible bull of opposition by the horns when I told the world some fifteen years later I was going to make a fiddle."

When he had finished his education, and before he began to earn his own livelihood, he employed his

time in writing verse, and in experimenting with the
tonal qualities of different kinds of wood. In the course
of his experiments he hit upon a contrivance by means
of which the usual volume of sound produced by the
Aeolian harp could be more than quadrupled. He
developed quite a passion for the use of keen edged
tools,—a passion made all-too-manifest by the trade
mark which he left on nearly every article of furniture
in the house, much to the disgust of his sisters.
The number of curios in the shape of work-boxes,
brackets, and other nicknacks which he made in a few
months would have sufficed to decorate the window of
a respectable toyshop.

But the carving tools had to be set aside for a while.
Walter was now seventeen, almost full-grown, and
ready to begin life's battle. He was apprenticed to the
Messrs. J. & A. Phillips & Co., of Manchester, an
honourable firm of merchants, with whom he served
five years. During his leisure moments, however, he
paid much attention to literature, and especially to
music. His youngest sister, Mary Ann, had married the
organist and composer Joseph Thorne Harris, only
son of J. J. Harris, for many years organist of the
Cathedral, Manchester. With the Harrises Mayson was
on the most intimate terms, spending nearly all his
spare evenings at their house, where his taste for
classical and chamber music was encouraged and
developed. It was suggested by Mr. Harris that he
should become his pupil, but it appears that the
suggestion was never acted upon. Up to this time

Mayson had scarcely seen and certainly had never handled that which at a later period was to be the idol of his life—a fiddle. But an interesting example of the luthier's art came unexpectedly into his possession. He was much run down in health, and his employers very generously sent him on holiday to the Lake country for three months. Somebody told him that his grandfather William Green's fiddle was still in existence, and for sale. Mayson rushed away in quest of the owner, struck a bargain, and carried the treasure away jubilantly. The instrument, which possessed a beautiful tone, was labelled " Jacob Stainer," but was really a fine specimen of the work of Richard Duke. The contemplation of its graceful lines and " sweet " varnish roused his poetic nature as it had never been roused before. " I could never look at or handle that fiddle," he writes, " but that I was agitated through and through, and my hands twitched nervously so that I feared the instrument would slip to the ground." Mayson now took lessons in violin playing, and after a few years' constant practice he mastered the technique of the instrument. His grandfather's fiddle was his inseparable companion for many years, but alas! there is an ebb as well as a flow in the tide of men's affairs. In an evil hour the " Duke " was ruthlessly taken from its owner for a debt which he did not incur. Gradually, change upon change took place in the home of the Maysons, and when Walter was twenty-one, the first great sorrow broke in upon the happy family,— it was the death of the second son, William. Two

years later the youngest daughter, Sarah, darling of
the family, was laid to rest beside her brother, she
being but three weeks short of one and twenty
Mrs. Mayson was so stricken with sorrow that she
never lifted her head for months, and Walter was almost
broken-hearted, for he and his sister had been most
truly attached, and seldom out of reach of each other's
affection.

The break up of the family was now complete. Two
years after the death of Sarah, the father was brought
to his "long home," being followed at a short interval
by his daughter Elizabeth. Walter's brother and his
only-surviving sister, Jane, were now married, and he
was left alone with his mother. Sorrows oft-recurring
and so crushing as these could not have been borne
by so sensitive a nature as Walter Mayson's, but for
the solace of a mother's care, and the soothing influence
of his fiddle's melody. He could now play well, and
all his leisure moments were given to art—chiefly
musical art. He studied Beethoven and Mozart, he
wrote elegies and tragedies, and he had become a violin
collector on a small scale. About this time he fell in
love with, and began to pay his addresses to Catherine
May Elwood, eldest daughter of John Elwood, trumpeter
to Sir Charles Hallè, and bandmaster to the Earl of
Ellesmere. After a devoted courtship of six years, he
and Miss Elwood were married at Eccles Church, near
Manchester, on December 24th, 1863. But not for
long did Providence spare this good woman to the
young artist, for she died in premature childbirth

some six months after. Mayson's sorrow was great, but he made up his mind that as his line had not been cast in pleasant places he must bear his burden without a murmur. His mother was still with him, doing all she could to comfort him and to tone down the acute edges of his sorrow.

When he had got the better of his grief, and all-too soon, he fell in love with Elizabeth, widow of Frank King, of Manchester, whom he married, after a brief courtship, at S. Mary's Church, Higher Crumpsall, near Manchester, on June 20th, 1866. Mrs. King had one son and one daughter by her former husband, and Mayson adopted both, thus increasing his responsibility and expense threefold in one day—a thing ill-warranted by his slender income. The earlier years of their married life were spent by Walter and Elizabeth Mayson at Cheetham Hill, where were born to them three children—Sarah Elizabeth, Walter Henry, and Stansfield. After six years spent in tolerable comfort they removed to The Polygon, Lower Broughton, near Manchester, where was born to them another child, Florence Gertrude, and where was fashioned, in the back attic of the same house, that first fiddle by our artist, which was to herald on a career of, we think, as signal a devotion to Art, and as dogged a determination to succeed in its pursuit, as history can furnish.

Chapter 3.

Taking up the Gouge.

THE passion for the fiddle had so grown upon Mayson at the age of thirty-nine that he resolved to buy a quantity of maple and pine, merely to have the pleasure of looking at that which *could* be made into such masterpiece of form and sound-producing mechanism, never for a moment dreaming of attempting to construct an instrument. But in the early autumn of 1873, whilst fondly handling the slabs of wood, he wondered, "Why not try my hand at fiddle-making?" He could only fail, at the worst, he mused, though failure had never been one of his weaknesses. He resolved to try, got books on the subject, blocks made, &c., and, as Mr. J. Broadhouse observes in an article on the subject, "told his friends he was going to make a fiddle." Of course, some people smiled at such a project, others sneered, and all looked coldly on what they considered to be a passing whim of a somewhat erratic mind. Who ever heard of a man taking up the gouge at his age and succeeding in the delicate art of violin making? Even those who were apprenticed to the profession from youth seldom made headway and no modern maker ever turned out work that would compare with the masterpieces of the old Italians. The idea was absurd. Mayson himself had serious doubts, and would, perhaps, have dismissed the idea as an idle dream, but for the persistence with which some of his friends maintained that modern fiddles could not be made that would stand the test of comparison with Cremonese instruments. Antagonism is often an important element of development, calling into action resources of character that would for ever lie dormant in the background of consciousness but for its ministry. "I remember very well," says Mr. Mayson, "one evening, two of my Job's comforters calling upon me and speaking disparagingly of modern art, in the presence of myself and my mother (who always lived with me), and how I gave my leg a sounding slap, saying, that I *would* make a fiddle, and, before I had done with the business, would make them all acknowledge I could. It was then my mother uttered those words of faith which I never tire of repeating—words which John Ruskin would have gone far to hear—'What Walter says he will do, you may be certain he *will*' a few words, but of sublime confidence in me, and words which put strength into me to attempt the Stradivarian task. I was determined to succeed, if for no other reason than that she should not have to admit misplaced confidence, and I thank God that she lived to see me do great work, which she gloried in. I shall never forget her joy on each occasion when telegrams came from various Exhibitions announcing

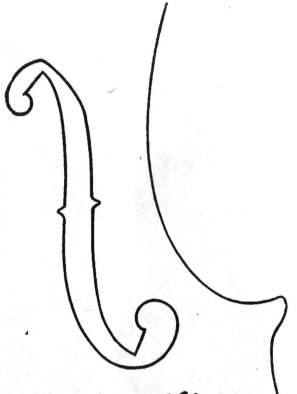

Soundhole of Violin.
No 1, Oct. 1873, Fig 1.

MAYSON'S FIRST VIOLIN.

that I had been awarded medals." So Mayson took
up the gouge and made his first fiddle. The event
was the turning point of his life, and we cannot do
better than give the main facts in his own words. " Well
then," he writes, "it was on the 16th October, 1873,
that I jointed back and belly of my No. 1 fiddle;
yes! and the joints were by no means bad, and show
out well to-day, for the instrument is left by Will
to my son Stansfield, and so is ever by us. It is on
the lines of "Joseph" and eminently the work of an
amateur—a lover of what he does I take that to mean
—and fairly well finished, purfled, and covered with
amber coloured oil varnish. From the very first I was
determined to use no spirit varnish,—that would-be
destroyer of all good tone. The tone of my No. 1
was only moderately powerful, but the quality was
good, and one George Crompton said I should never
make a better instrument. Absurd! My mother said
he did not want me to."

It will be observed from the accompanying illustrations
that the lines of Mayson's first instrument, although
reminiscent of those of Guarneri, are really original,
and that they evince much strength of conception.
The soundholes are too vigorous to be graceful, and the
angularity of the upper arch can only be described as
a rather grotesque exaggeration of the quasi-Gothic
curve of Joseph. Nevertheless the *tout-ensemble*
impresses one with that chic and absence of conventionality
which is all-too rare a characteristic of modern work.
The soundhole is an index to the mind of the man.

Mayson was no copyist. He could not copy if he tried, and he bungled most where he copied best. During what may be described as his second period he made a few Strad copies, which were positive failures, both artistically and acoustically. Sir William Hamilton says that mimicry is a gift which is most marked in people who lack originality and the power of initiative, and is altogether absent in men of great intellectual powers. Mayson discovered at the outset wherein his power lie, and he knew what he must not as well as what he must attempt to do. None could say with greater truth than he that he applied to his own faculties the touch-stone of Socrates.

Mayson's first fiddle was lauded by all, and borrowed right and left, and if he had had a weak head he would, in all probability, have been spoilt for future work, and would have missed doing what one is proud to think is among the best examples of the luthier's art. But he got to work in earnest, as indeed he was obliged to, for about this time he was discharged from the shipping house where he had worked hard and long, in order that room might be made for—Germany!

Life's battle had begun for Walter Mayson now in all its grim reality. He had to face the responsibility of providing for a growing family with a diminishing income. He took a room in Barton Arcade, Deansgate, Manchester, where he set up, before he had made ten fiddles, as a professional violin maker and repairer—a presumptuous thing to do, it must be admitted.

Mr. James Fildes was the first to bring patronage to the humble *atelier* of Barton Arcade. He bought Mayson's No. 2 fiddle, for which he paid £10, remarking that he would readily give £50 for the first fiddle of the artist's make which he should consider to be worth that sum. These words, coming as they did from an honest heart and a keen connoisseur, gave the violin maker no small encouragement.

The gouge proved unequal to the task of providing for the needs of a big family, and the service of the pen was therefore frequently requisitioned. Mr. Mayson wrote a great deal, some of his essays and songs being published in the leading Manchester papers. He published five of his dramas for private circulation. These, although not without some literary merit, are long since cast into obscurity. As an example of his style at this period, the following little essay, selected from his unpublished remains, may be taken:

"EULOGIUM FIDIS.

Andrew Fletchei, of Saltoun, in a letter to the Marquis of Montrose wrote : 'I know a very wise man that believed that if a man were permitted to write all the ballads he need not care who should make the laws of a nation." And history shows that the story of the British people is largely the story of their ballads. Now ballads have been invariably wedded to song, and song from time immemorial has been accompanied by the strains of musical instruments. The inference is not illogical, therefore, that the story of a nation is in some measure the story of its musical instruments. Even as the cephalic, vertical, orbital, prognathistic, and other indices of the skull enable the anthropologist to determine the ethnic relationship of prehistoric and existing races, so do the forms and sounds of musical instruments guide the musical antiquary in determining the aesthetic status of the people who invented them. The mysticism of ancient Egypt is typified by the sistrum, an instrument which the Egyptians played in the ceremonies accompanying the worship of Isis. Plutarch says 'the shaking of the four bars within the four circular apsis of the sistrum represented the agitation of the four elements within the compass of the world, by which all things are continually destroyed and reproduced, and that the cat sculptured upon the apsis was an emblem of the moon.' This is nothing less than a musical symbol of the philosophy of the land of the Pharaohs. The blasting buccina and the clattering crotalum were characteristic of the Roman thirst for empire. The lyra and sambuca as modified and developed by the Greeks were typical of Greek culture and refinement. The harp of the bard told the tale of the Briton who rushed at his foe with rage boiling in his veins, at the same time that it told of the bard's real business of milking his goats and cultivating the mysteries of the grove. The Highland bagpipe imprisons in its cavities the fiend of bloody feud, and its wail is like that of the ghost of an old yew tree in pain. How true to the story of the clans! From the skull-drum of primitive savagery down to the brass-band of modern militarism, history is writ large in the forms and sounds of musical instruments. The fiddle is the child of the Renaissance, and its message is appreciated in proportion as the inner meaning of that Force is understood. The great, brooding spirit which produced Michael Angelo, the artist, Erasmus, the man of letters, Reuchlin, the savant, Luther the reformer, and Moore, the Utopian, also begat Gaspara da Salo, Maggini, Amati, Stradivari, Guarneri, and Bergonzi, the fiddle makers. The Sistine frescoes, the 'De Libero Arbitrio,' the 'Utopia,' nay the Reformation was no greater event than was the advent of the King of instruments. The fiddle represents, so far, the highest achievement of the science and art of musical instrument making, and that chiefly, no doubt, because its tones approach to the perfection of the human voice more nearly than do those of any other musical instrument. But great fiddles would be meaningless and useless without great fiddle players. The story of these last is as important as the story of the great statesmen, philosophers, and scientists of a country, for even as it is the business of such to guide and edify, so it is the business of *virtuosi* to refine the manners and delight the minds of their fellow-men. To hear *virtuosi* is a privilege granted to the few, but the fairs, wakes, and dances of our countryside have their fiddlers, so that where the *virtuoso* charms his thousands, the humble minstrel or strolling fiddler charms his tens of thousands. The fiddle is essentially an instrument of peace; its notes are wholly unadapted to martial strains. And although in days gone by it not infrequently was associated with the Bacchanalia of the ale-house, yet there is not the slightest doubt that even the loquacious toper was more amenable to suasion when reason expressed itself in the language of the fiddle.

Sweet fiddle! It laughs with the mirthful maiden on the village green, it weeps with the widow in the wake, and it mingles its voice with that of the old precentor in the solemn Te Deum. Who can tell the power of the fiddle for good; who recount the blood-less victories it has won? The days of the countryside fiddler are nearly over, and his place is being usurped by the organ grinder and other noisy intruders. Already

the days of innocent merriment are among the days
that return no more.

> Alas for the days of fiddle-de-dee,
> And the youths who danced so merrily."

When Mayson was in a good position with a large
firm of merchants, and able to entertain freely, there
were any number of flatterers who were anxious to
say nice things to him about his hobby, but when it came
to be a question of associating with or encouraging a
fiddle maker, it was another matter, and the poor
artist had to rest content with the society of the
faithful few. He felt the slight very much, and mused
ruefully how the progress of art was retarded by the
cold and even cruel conduct of people who called themselves friends, but whose friendship was only from the
teeth out. He was not cast down, however, for he was
doing no mean work, and he felt strong and happy
in the consciousness of duty well performed. A friend
of his in London—Mr. William Pickering—showed some
of his work to the great William Ebsworth Hill, who at
once said "This man is a born fiddle maker, and it is
really refreshing to find, in these days of copying, one
who dares to be original. If I had this man for
three months he would beat B——— and the rest of
them into mummies." The words, coming as they did
from one who was recognized as the greatest expert
in Europe at the time, greatly cheered the despised
artist. They would probably have inflated men less
gifted than Mayson with vanity, but they only spurred
our artist to greater activity and incited him to renew

THE POLYGON, LOWER BROUGHTON, WHERE MAYSON MADE HIS FIRST FIDDLE.

the vow of humility. He wrote in a note book in which
he had pinned Mr. Pickering's letter the following
words: "Now, I think very strongly with Mr. Ruskin,
that all great work,—art work especially—must be
approached with great humility, because (as has been
the case with me) the least leaning to pride over fancied
excellence is invariably visited by a reverse. And this
is as it should be, for the artist must not work for
aggrandisement of self, but for the glory of art and
the good of posterity. Should a line or a curve, or
arrangement of thickness please the eye or assist to
procure a finer tone, by all means draw, carve, or
caliper to produce them, but do it modestly, humbly,
and with love; so that if you go down to the grave
poor, slighted, and worn-out with toil, it may yet be
said of you, 'he laboured for us and in singleness of
heart, and we love his work and his memory.'"

So Mayson braced himself for earnest work and further
excellence, and was on the road, it was fondly thought,
to achieve early success and a sure competence. But a
dark cloud suddenly loomed on the horizon, which was
to hide the face of prosperity's sun. It happened that
one of the sons of a numerous family of violin makers
came to reside in Manchester, and then Mayson had to
go to the wall with a vengeance. Not only luke-warm
friends, but those who had been counted among the few
tried friends abandoned the poor artist, so that he was now
left alone as a pelican in the wilderness, or as a sparrow
on the house-top. It was said that all his work was
wrong, and it was prophesied that he would die in

the workhouse.   The person to whom the latter remark was made replied "Mayson may die in the workshop, but never in the workhouse."   But it seemed as though the beginning of the end had come, and to ward off present monetary troubles, Mayson made a fatal mistake: he sent about twenty of his violins to Messrs. Puttick and Simpson's auction room, where they were sold for little more than the wood had cost him. This angered many who had paid him fair prices, and lost him patron after patron.   But what could he do? Become bankrupt, with money in his work by him?   That he could not nor would, so he had recourse to a desperate expedient.   Difficulties and troubles were warded off only for a time however; the inevitable had to come, and Mayson was obliged to go into a humbler workshop, his stepson, Frank King, going with him and assisting him in the business.   A move was made to Prestwich, where, by hard work and economical living, some of the lost ground was gradually recovered. Things taking a better turn, another remove was made to Cheetham Hill, where, in an ill-advised moment, Mayson resolved to build a house through a building society. It is marvellous what momentous issues often hang on a single moment or thought.   The decision to build a house through a building society cost Mayson the peace of mind and earthly comforts of a life-time, as we shall see later on.   Soon after removing to Cheetham Hill, the family was cast into sorrow by the death of Frank King, Mayson's stepson, who was greatly beloved by the artist and idolized by his mother. Following upon

sorrow came trouble. Sales again fell off, and strive as
he would, it became impossible for the poor artist to
keep up the monthly payments to the building society.

Chapter 4.

The Fiddles of the Lake.

IN the year 1881 Mayson sold his house at Cheetham Hill and removed to Newby Bridge, close to Windermere, Lake Side, where he rented an old house to which was attached a fine fruit and flower garden. He vacated this at the end of the year, removing to Croft House, a beautifully kept and well-situated cottage, near the lake. Here he remained for six years, writing verse and carving fiddles, turning out work that in centuries to come will make his name famous as one of England's greatest artists. After paying the back instalments on the house at Cheetham Hill, and discharging other debts, he had only £6 left, with tools, wood, and a little furniture, to start with at Lake Side. Some hard things were said about him in connection with this removal to an obscure district, but it may be urged in justification thereof that he had already earned some reputation, and could consquently do business by correspondence just as well as if he had remained in a busy town. What is more, he could live at rather less than half the cost of town life, with the addition of pure air and beautiful scenery as a gift. Besides, how carry on business again where sales by auction had taken place? To stay in Manchester was obviously impossible to a man of the fine susceptibilities and delicate self-respect of Mayson.

During the years 1881—1888, Mayson turned out on an average about two instruments per month. A tolerably clear idea of the progress he had made in the art may be gathered from the accompanying illustrations.

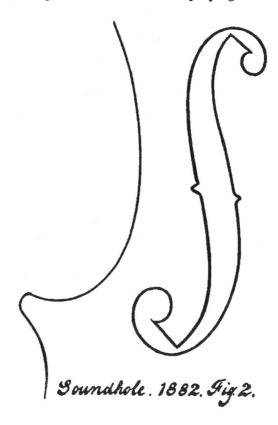

Soundhole. 1882. Fig 2.

The measurements he adopted at this period differed only very slightly from those of Stradivari. The wood which he used for his best instruments was excellent, but he was sometimes obliged to use indifferent material for his second-class instruments. The arching was a trifle flatter than that of the grand Strad, and considerably flatter than that which he himself adopted at a later period. He varied his thicknesses in almost every instrument, a fact which proves that he had not at this time emerged from the experimental stage. He had no fixed outline for his sound-hole also, minute differences being observable in almost every specimen which belong to this period. . He tried different sizes, inclinations, and positions, with a view no doubt of arriving at certain knowledge of the subtle relation existing between the sound-holes and the tone. His varnish is of excellent quality, mostly of deep golden amber colour, and perfectly transparent and elastic. The tone is usually grand and flute-like, but is occasion-ally deficient in the silvery clearness and sweetness which characterizes that ot the later instruments. A fiddle made by Mayson at the end of this period, named "Cordelia," is as fine an example of the luthier's art as any I have ever seen. Wood, varnish, and workmanship are the acme of perfection, and the tone is large, rich, and free as the tone of a Peter van den Gheyn bell. If this fiddle had been made in the workshop of Stradivari, it would sell at a fabulous sum, but because it has been made at a humble workshop in prosaic Britain it may never realize the price of a modern German pianoforte. Britons, it would seem, can never be induced to accept as work of art that which is not of foreign workmanship.

Mayson loved not only his art, but also the offspring of his art, and, like Turner, he never parted with his best work till compelled to by the force of circumstances. There were about a dozen instruments in his cabinet which he would not part with for any sum. These he never showed to any except his bosom friends, and he resisted some tempting offers for them, even at periods when it was known to a few that he was in dire straits. He kept "Cordelia" in a small cabinet in his workshop for eleven years, merely to have the delight of looking at it every now and again, when he would be lost in contemplation of its matchless form and colour. During one of these spells of rapture he wrote the following stanzas, in which are some lines that would bring no discredit to the pen of a Swinburne or a Watson.

THE FIDDLE.

So elegant in line, with softest curve,
  In flames enveloped which do never die;
Though fragile as the tissue of a nerve,
  Thou'rt strong in grace and beauty, which the eye
Does never weary, ever seeks again,
And lingers long on what 'twill long retain.

Strange, that the sordid can ethereal rise—
   Absorb the mind of him who, loving, makes!
As his deft genius quickly o'er flies!
   How it rewards him by the shape it takes!
For Galatea Pygmalion craved a soul:
Here sculpture soul and body does unroll.

Light and a shade commingle and embrace,
   And undulation, well defined and free,
Sinks on a movement, and there's just a trace
   Of that which looked a bold declivity ;
But, make another movement, and behold !
New lines and curves and flames we see unfold.

To him, whose eye is only for thy grace,
   Thy fascinating charms would seem to be
But for that eye to take from place to place,
   Recurring ever to its memory,
Forgetful that a soul so mighty lives
Within the shell that so much rapture gives.

The Muse is wiser, and, with tender hand,
   Lingers on chords she, tremblingly, evokes ;
But, inspiration lending her command,
   What pathos from that soul flies with the strokes !
The air is palpitating with strains,
And long their purity the earth retains.

'Tis when the billow rolls upon the shore
   And is, by impact, stranded—eddies—dies,
We fail to grasp that what was grand before
   Should in a moment lie, no more to rise :
But that we sing defies all earth's abuse ;
In age 'tis mightiest ; injured, most in use.

Gently, with rev'rence, thou art laid aside,
 And none are worse, how many better for
The themes which laughed and danced and almost cried
 As they from such a wonder wildly soar !
Yet, when again we look on thee at rest,
Do we thy soul or body love the best ?

In 1883 Mayson exhibited a case of violins at the
Cork Exhibition, and in 1885 a quartette at the In-
ventions, London, for both of which he received a
silver medal. In 1888 he exhibited a case of violins
at the Melbourne Exhibition, for which he was awarded
the gold medal—a trophy which he never received,
owing to the affair going into bankruptcy. In the
Cork and London awards an originality in edging was
specially mentioned, being described as a "graceful
ornamentation in the form of a Grecian ogee between
the purfling and the rims."

Mr. Mayson never exhibited instruments after 1888;
he had, it would appear, lost confidence in the ability,
or integrity, or both, of musical juries. He often
quoted the award at the great International Exhibition
of 1851 as an instance of flagrant miscarriage of
justice, when J. B. Vuillaume was adjudged to be the
winner of the grand council medal. The jury on the
violins in that Exhibition consisted of thirteen men,
only one of whom could play the fiddle ! It is not
to be wondered at that the "merits" rewarded by
such a jury were said to be: "New modes of making
violins in such a manner that they are matured and

CROFT HOUSE, WINDERMERE, MAYSON'S RESIDENCE FROM 1882 TO 1888.

perfected immediately on the completion of the manu-
facture, thus avoiding the necessity of keeping them
for considerable periods to develop their excellencies."

In the year 1887 business became again so slack
with Mayson that he almost despaired of being able
to continue his work.   He had not sold a single
instrument for nine months, and he had spent his
last penny on a supply of timber for future use.
But help came quite unexpectedly.   The family were
one day—one out of many—about to sit down to a
more than usually frugal dinner, when a rather startling
knock came to the door, and two gentlemen from
Liverpool asked to see Mr. Mayson.   They had come
to see his fiddles and would buy if they could be
suited.   They were shown a number of instruments,
and after a lengthened trial of their respective merits,
selected one, for which they paid £20 in cash.   The
despondent artist looked gratefully at the gold being
deposited on the table, at the same time brushing
away the furtive tears that stole down his cheeks.   The
gold meant bread at least for a few months longer.

*   *   *   *   *   *   *   *   *

The rest of this chapter can be best told in Mr.
Mayson's own words.   *   *   *   *   " But the incubus
of the house I had built at Manchester," he wrote,
" still clung to me, for, of course, I was liable at any
moment to be called upon to meet any and all losses,

and much correspondence had already passed between
me and the building society on the subject; but the
end was not yet. Another and a greater affliction
now overwhelmed me: my mother was no more. At
the venerable age of 85 she passed to a rest which
was well-earned,—if ever purity of life *can* earn anything in this world for enjoyment in the next—with
all her faculties undimmed; blessing me and my work
as she wished me 'good night' for ever. She lies
in the yard of the ancient Church mentioned before
(which is mentioned in my novel 'The Stolen Fiddle'
and which was written here), and I thought, when
leaving her in the cold, sad silence, and utterly
by her dear self amongst the strange dead, that my
heart was too full for more sorrow or world-hardness
to enter it: but I was mistaken. In a while after
this, I was peremptorily written to by the building
society to the effect that, if no interest were forth-
coming for the lease on the house, or I did not take
it up or enter it as tenant (the former tenant having
left), the house would be sold at once, and I should
have to make good any loss by such sale. I met this
demand in the best way I could: my wife and the
two younger girls went and lived in the house, and
I got leave to vacate the one we lived in with the
others as soon as I had settled matters up. It was
a hard day's work for me when 1 had to leave this
exceedingly lovely country, my mother's grave, and the
sweet associations that had sprung up and grown
around me. How I recalled incident after incident of

my life there, and thought upon thought, as I saw different features of the peaceful landscape pass before me on my last journey from Croft House in the conveyance that brought me to the station. But the most trying ordeal of all was the last glimpse of the quaint old Church Tower. My spirit lingered long beside a certain grave under its shade—a grave to which it has journeyed a thousand times since. Thus it was that I left Lake Side, the loveliest spot in all England, and the dearest to me."

MAYSON AT THE AGE OF 55.

Chapter 5.

BACK IN MANCHESTER.

VERY soon Mayson was at sea once more in his native town. He rigged up a workshop in an upper-room in the house which he had built, and plodded away diligently if drearily at his beloved art. He managed just to eke out a bare existence, but could not meet the demands of the building society, so at the end of eighteen months he was obliged to vacate the house and remove to Oxford Road, Manchester, where he remained from 1890 till his death in 1904. The period covered by this chapter embraces the decade from 1889 to 1899—from the time when Mr. Mayson returned to Manchester to the time when he opened a branch in London. This decade may be conveniently described as Mayson's second period, and to it must be assigned the greater part of the artist's best work. He now made on an average one instrument per week. He was a rapid worker, albeit an exceptionally careful one. He would go over the tables of his high-class instruments fifteen or twenty times, gauging and working the thicknesses to the nth, according to the principle of graduation which he had adopted. He was wont to say that "at a push" he could make from first to last four scrolls a day, allowing three hours for each scroll, but that it was his rule never to "throw" more than one scroll in the same day, owing to the mental and nervous fatigue which the work involved. Sound-hole cutting was his chief delight. He would sometimes spend half a day in carefully cutting the ff, paying due regard to the angle of inclination in its relation to the model. There was, in fact, no part of the work to which he paid such exact attention as this. But a careful analysis of a typical instrument will be given at a later stage; let this suffice for the present.

In the year 1893 matters brightened a little with our artist. All his children were now grown up, two of the sons had started on their own account in the musical profession, Stansfield doing particularly well as a violin teacher, and the daughters attended to the shop, where were sold general intruments, strings, fittings, and other musical odds and ends. A gentleman residing at Gothenberg, Sweden, placed an order with Mayson for a high-class quartette, stipulating that the instruments be named "Haydn," "Mozart,' "Schubert," and "Beethoven"; the price fixed upon being £75, plus a Joseph son of Andrew Guarnerius violin of excellent preservation. The order naturally created no small stir in the violin world, and attention was directed afresh to the work of the despised artist· Three other big orders came to hand in the same year, and Mayson was at length able to stock his *atelier* with the best kind of wood, which he imported direct from Italy and the Tyrol. The timber thus obtained at great cost and trouble he strictly reserved for his finest . instruments. And here it would not be out of place, perhaps, to remark that it is a thousand pities that artists of the calibre of Mayson should be constrained by circumstances to use any but the best material. The great Cremonese never used any but the best material, or at least the best procurable, nor did they turn out instruments of inferior workmanship. They did not arrange their work into classes, according to material and style, but turned out work of one class, for which they charged the highest price they could get. It has happened times out of number that the lower priced instruments of Mayson have got to the market, or otherwise changed hands, when they have been sold at from £4 to £6, with the result that the reputation of the artist has suffered considerably. I have seen instruments bearing his label which, in point of tone, were little if any better than the ordinary trade fiddle. In these cases the material was invariably to blame. There is an almost unpardonable disparity between the tonal merits of Mayson's No. 1 and No. 5 styles. It is, as I said, matter of profound regret that the good man was at all obliged to use indifferent material. What could he not have accomplished if he had been in easy circumstances, with all the sylvan wealth of an Alpine forest within his reach? Well may an Angelo sculpture his "David" with his chisel furrowing the breast of an immaculate slab of marble, but an Angelo could not bestow divinity on a grey dolmen. Well may a Sir Joshua mix his matchless carnation with pure pigments and an honest vendor only a few yards down the street; but what could he or a greater than he do in these days of cheap adulteration ?

The brief flash of prosperity induced Mayson to issue a new price list, which I reproduce here, both on account of the information it gives and of the interest which attaches to it as an epitome of contemporary opinion on his high class work.

PRICE LIST OF VIOLINS, &c.,

THE ENTIRE WORK OF

WALTER H. MAYSON,

62, Oxford Street, Manchester.

TERMS NET CASH.

VIOLINS, STYLE No. 1.

Made of Good old Sycamore and Pine, flat
edges, purfled, and varnished £5 0 0

STYLE No. 2.

The same, with raised edges and better wood   7 10 0

STYLE No. 3.

Fine Maple or Sycamore, and better finished   10 0 0

STYLE No. 4.

Made of Choice Wood, and fine finish.........   12 10 0

STYLE No. 5.

Made of the very Finest Wood, and finished
in a style to bear comparison with any ...   15 0 0

"STRAD," "GUARNERIUS," and "MAYSON" MODELS.

VIOLAS, one-third extra.

VIOLONCELLOS, from £20 to £35.

THREE PRIZE MEDALS:

Cork, 1883. | Inventions, 1885. | Melbourne, 1888 .

" CORDELIA " FECIT 1889,

From *Musical Opinion*, May 1, 1888: "We have inspected Mayson's Violins, which are exceedingly handsome and beautifully made; and we are pleased to see such perfection arrived at by an English maker. They will doubtless rank amongst the highest class instruments of the future."

From *Railway Supply Journal*, April 13, 1889: "The verdict on Mayson's Violins is indisputable. The only English maker who received a medal at Cork, 1883, and at Melbourne, 1888. His ambition is high and honourable." &c., &c., &c.

From *The Strad*, May, 1891: "We acknowledge receipt from Mr. W. H. Mayson, of Manchester, of a violin, * * * dated 1890. Mr. Mayson may well be proud of having turned out such an instrument. The workmanship is fine, the selection of the wood, the rich golden varnish, the shape of the *f* holes, all prove that the maker must be a thorough master of his art. The tone is exceptionally fine, especially on the E and A strings. If Mr. Mayson continues to turn out such work, his violins may, indeed, one day replace the masterpieces of some of the old Italian makers, which must one of these days become a thing of the past."

Shortly after the appearance of the article in the "Strad," Mayson made a fiddle on which he expended more care and time than usual, and he conceived the audacious (?) notion of presenting it to Lady Hallè. When the instrument was completed it was submitted to a few connoisseurs for their opinion; all of whom agreed that it was of matchless perfection as regards workmanship and that it possessed a remarkably fine tone. The fiddle was duly presented,

through Sir Charles Hallè, by letter, but its receipt
was not even acknowledged. Mayson went to the
trouble of enquiring by messenger whether the violin
had been safely received, but he was vouchsafed no
reply. Shortly after, Sir Charles Hallè took occasion
to remark publicly at a rehearsal that he and Lady
Hallè were greatly annoyed at the impertinence of
certain people who had made bold to send an instrument for their acceptance !

This sounds almost incredible, but the story is
absolutely authentic. Compare with this incident the
fate of the Strad which was offered to Her Ladyship
by the Duke of Edinburgh. Mayson's part in this
little episode might have been lacking in the artificial
charm of etiquette, but it had the unction of purity
of heart and disinterestedness. Let the anathemas of
future ages avenge the pain of the poor artist ! The
world has not forgotten that the Emperor Leopold
lost his one chance of immortality when he refused
to render Jacob Stainer pecuniary assistance in his
hour of need. The Nemesis of history is very just.

Mr. Mayson himself forgot the rebuff in a very
short time. His admiration for Lady and Sir Charles
Hallè was so genuine and deep-rooted that he had
forgiven their cold treatment of him in less time
than it took to varnish a fiddle. Patient humility and
eager forgivingness were outstanding traits of his
character. Never did a man breathe who was more
ready than he to make ample amends for any wrong

unwittingly committed. He often feared that he had not forgiven certain things with that true-hearted thoroughness demanded by the Christ, and he would engage in serious searching of heart.

To convince himself that he was still a sincere admirer of Sir Charles Hallè, he set about to construct a special instrument, which was to be dedicated to the great man's memory. It was soon completed, and a marvellous example of the luthier's art it was. A lengthy notice of this instrument appeared in the issue of the "Violin Times" for April, 1896, which I reproduce *in extenso*, together with the illustrations. The article is from the pen of an eminent expert and author, and is as just as it is enthusiastic.

THE "HALLE-MAYSON" VIOLIN.

With this number we give an illustration (back and front) of this destined-to-be historical violin, by Walter H. Mayson, Manchester. A well-known connoisseur writes : "It has been specially constructed in memory of the celebrated Manchester musician and conductor, the late Sir Charles Hallè; and a careful examination of it convinces me that it is in every way a worthy *souvenir* of the man in whose honour it has been made; and, indeed, that the 'Hallè-Mayson' ranks as one of the highest creations of the Luthier's art. In appearance it somewhat resembles the grand Strad model—it is not too flat—but its corners, though giving every indication of strength and solidity, are rather more extended. The materials used in its construction are of the best, whether in regard to artistic effect, or acoustic quality. The figure of the back is

THE "HALLE-MAYSON" VIOLIN, FECIT 1895.

.broad, giving to the instrument a very dignified and noble appearance. The ribs are full and strong, and the front table is about the grandest bit of pine I have ever seen. Its 'reed' is of medium width, shewing here and there .beautiful feathery flashes. The modelling is exquisite, its flowing curves seeming actually to idealize that which artistes term 'The line of beauty.' In my hearing a very skilful expert said : ' This is calculated to throw lustre even on MAYSON's fame ! ' The purfling is excellent, the sound holes graceful and beautifully cut, and the scroll, noble and massive, bears itself as befits the real ' aristocracy of fiddles ! ' The varnish in which it is enshrined, is similar in character and quality to that used by the best of old masters, and its colour brown-red orange—seems to change like the chameleon with every varying light in which it may be placed, and even in semi-darkness it collects the struggling rays of light, and reflects them like a prism or diamond ! In the place where the label is usually fixed, it bears the inscription—

'IN MEMORIAM,
Sir Charles Hallè,
Obit, 1895.'

and beneath the other sound hole,

' Walter H. Mayson,
Fecit Manchester,'

in Manuscript.

In this instrument there is none of that mechanical ' finicking' non-intelligent reproduction of other makers' forms and models, but the whole work is highly original, artistic and individualistic ; and it is only fair to say that this remark equally applies to all this maker's instruments.

The same hand who made the ' Hallè ' will make others ; but it is hard to believe that it will ever produce any that can possibly eclipse this particular instrument in any essential of the violin makers' art.

But as I have hitherto only referred to this violin
from the fancier's standpoint, common fairness compels
me to say, that it is equally desirable from the player's.
The tone is full, mellow and pleasing, alike in the
higher and lower positions. *It sings, but never howls!*
Thus Science and Art have gone hand-in-hand, and, in

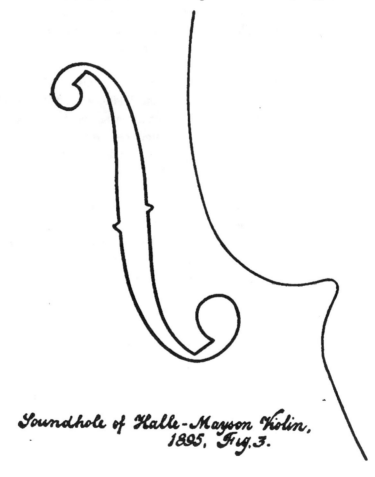

*Soundhole of Halle-Mayson Violin,
1895, Fig. 3.*

conjunction have conspired to delight the eye, charm the
ear and wake the soul to rapture; and even Time, the
destroyer of all things, will, in this case, delay its final
purpose, and lend a helping hand to enhance its beauties
and perfect its qualities."

The outline, inclination, &c., of the sound-hole of
the Hallè-Mayson violin are shown in the opposite
illustration, which is reproduced from a rubbing, fig. 3.

Very fine instruments of this period are " Old
Windsor," a carved back fiddle, and " Queen Victoria,"
a magnificent fiddle which was made specially to the
order of Miss Evangeline Anthony, the talented
daughter of the Editor and part-proprietor of the
" Hereford Times," who is now recognized as one of the
leading lady *virtuosi*. These instruments are shown
in the accompanying illustrations. With regard to the
carved-back instruments, it is to be observed that the
carving is in bass-relief, the raised surface being only
about one-fortieth of an inch, but the effect is wonderful for so slight a cutting.

And here once again we must " open a dark saying
on the harp," this time to conclude the sad story of
Mayson's troubles with the building society before
referred to. The artist shall speak for himself. He
writes : " But all this time a final settlement with
the building society was in abeyance; for I had
brought matters no nearer a satisfactory end by leaving
the premises at Crumpsall, rather had I put them
back. So one morning I received a letter from the

"QUEEN ALEXANDRA," VIOLIN.

" OLD WINDSOR," FECIT 1893.

" QUEEN ALEXANDRA," VIOLIN'

society's lawyers informing me that the property had
been sold at a heavy loss, and I was requested to
make good the said loss forthwith. This staggered me
outright, for it would have taken most of all I had
to realize half of the amount at a forced sale. So,
at my wits' end, I did what I am humble enough
to admit I have often done—I fell on my knees for
guidance, and did not ask in vain. On staring the
position in the face, I decided to adopt the course
of begging the people to accept instalments of £5
per month—a course to which they agreed—and £135
out of the £150 loss was punctually so paid by me;
the society, in acknowledgment of my probity and of
my heavy previous loss, remitting £15, with a few
nice words of approbation. * * * Now I have
dealt at length with this episode in my life, as it
goes to show how I erred in first building the house,
and how doom ever hanged over my head thereafter.
But Providence tempered justice with mercy, in that
the whole of the penalty was not visited upon me
at once."

Chapter 6.

In London.

MR. MAYSON had yet (as events proved) to commit the greatest error of his life. This was no less than the extremely presumptuous act of opening a branch workshop in—of all places in the world—London, where fiddle makers and fiddle shops are as numerous as church steeples. For a man at his age (he was now sixty-four), and of his wordly substance, to expect to succeed in such a venture implied belief in the possibility of a trade miracle. Commercial miracles do happen, no doubt, but never in the fiddle world—at least not now-a-days. The days when a Vuillaume could by sound business methods, and a somewhat less sound moral methods, amass a rapid fortune, belonged to the earlier decades of the century that is past. When Mr. Mayson made known his intentions, he was seriously advised not to embark on any venture of the kind. But he was a man of many dreams, who loved to give his imagination the reins, and to indulge in wingless flights into the regions of the unknown. Genius is ever erratic: there is no calculating upon what it may or may not do to-morrow. Vincenzo Panormo opened in Paris yesterday, he is in London to-day, he may go to Ireland to-morrow, but who would be bold enough to predict where he will set up on the day after? Of Mayson it may be said, as it was said of Panormo: " He was of a restless temperament, which showed itself in continual self-imposed changes. He would not, or could not, permit his reputation to grow steadily, by residing long in one place, but as soon as fame was within his grasp, he sacrificed the work of years by removing to an entirely new field of labour." It must be admitted, however, that the migrations of Mayson were often due to circumstances over which he had no control. The stay in London lasted only three months and proved a calamitous failure, inasmuch as, in addition to causing a great business disappointment, it completely undermined a constitution already weakened by worries. Its story had better be told in Mayson's own words. " It was about the end of July, 1899, that I took a room on the second floor of No. 256 High Holborn, on the south side of the street, where I could secure a strong, steady north light. After considerable trouble I selected about thirty representative violins, from my accumulated stock at Manchester, and left that town alone, arriving in London, full of determination to do my best to arouse some sort of response, and open up a branch which should eventually develop into a good business. To set my new house in order was a labour of love, and it was soon apparent to a few very sterling friends who kept up correspondence with me that I meant business, as it was to the general public who only read my name in the window, that I did not. I stayed a few days with a bachelor friend, until I should secure lodgings in one of the outlying districts of London; for I thought, and rightly too, that moderate charges and fresh air would more than compensate for the cost of a contract ticket to and from one of the suburbs. For it was my intention to brave out loneliness and lack of such moderate comforts as home had afforded, and to endure any and every hardship for a few months; and, if naught came of the venture, to pack up and return to Manchester, having it in my power then to say to the London fiddle world, 'I came amongst you, bringing with me a certain reputation, and I put myself as prominently before you as my means would allow, silently claiming a hospitable welcome—but you did not respond.' During my stay with my bachelor friend, already referred to, and before I opened in High Holborn, I was seized with a sudden and severe illness, which nearly cost me my life. I was in bed for several days, being attended to by nobody but my friend, who watched by my bed day and night. My faithful friend Collins! I recovered in about a week, and returned to my workshop, but not feeling as strong as usual, it became necessary to secure lodgings where I could be attended to, if need be, and where I could have my meals properly cooked. Such lodgings were found in High Barnet, in Salisbury Road, where I stayed till my return home in November. I had

not been back to my workroom above a week when
I had another seizure. I with difficulty got into the
train, reached my lodgings, and went to bed, where
I remained for about ten days, being medically attended to and receiving every attention which kindness
could dictate. I gradually recovered my health and
strength, and at length I was able to go to my litte
sanctum in High Holborn.

Day after day crept on, but never a glimpse caught
I of the business I had so fondly hoped and believed
would come my way. I could scarcely comprehend
how it was that, out of so many people—not a few
of whom I had reckoned among my friends—not one
came to see me. Yes—I forget, one solitary friend
did call, it was Mr. Edward Heron-Allen—that prince
of writers on the king of instruments—and right glad
was I to see his kind face. I was sad and weary,
and my pocket grew lighter every day.

But a solace came in the delight I daily experienced
at Barnet. Morning saw me at breakfast at 7.30, and
in the station at 8.15; except in dull weather, when
the mornings were dark, which seldom happened in
Barnet. There the air is balmy as the breezes of
Gilead, and the sunshine undimmed as on the shores
of Carmel. The sky was bluer there than I saw
it anywhere else in England, as how otherwise could
it be, where the wind had swept over one hundred
miles of forest-clad country, unbroken by a hill or
mound? And the Barnet woods—those woods sacred

to the people from the days of Magna Charta—what solitude were they not the guardians of? Their refreshing shades, their exquisite oases,—sprinkled here and there like holy water on the tresses of a sculptured Madonna—what hypnotic repose were they not capable of bestowing on the weary mind? I often wandered away to a certain distant nook, where the berries were ripe, and the nuts hung in clusters within the reach of my hand, and I laid me down beside a solemn pool, where some friendly trees placidly trimmed their locks and viewed their lithe limbs in the huge mirror at their feet. * * * * I left London in November, a sadder and a wiser man. I made all necessary arrangements and returned to Manchester, where I shall probably remain for the rest short portion of the earthly journey."

It was a blessing in disguise for Mayson that the three months' stay in London proved barren and disappointing. Had he met there with the success he had vainly imagined would fall to his lot, he would have prolonged his stay in the metropolis. Such an event could have resulted in nothing but the gradual neglect of violin making, and the application to repairing and dealing as the sole means of livelihood. The musical atmosphere of London is fatal to the art of violin making. The greatest and the richest city in the world does not contain to-day half-a-dozen makers who can afford to devote the whole of their time to the construction of new violins. Stradivari himself would starve in modern London, unless he could make old

"Cremonas," and turn out factory fiddles at thirty shillings per dozen.

Mayson made only one high-class instrument whilst in London; this was "Elephanta,"—a fiddle to which he had only just put the finishing touches when Mr. Heron-Allen called on him on Nov. 1st, and which that well-known authority pronounced to be a "very fine" instrument. It has been impossible to obtain photographs of this fiddle, but the accompanying illustration, reproduced from a rubbing, will convey a correct idea of the size, form, and inclination of the soundholes. Soundholes are, as a rule, fair criteria of the artistic merits of the instruments to which they belong. If these are well cut, the probability is that the rest of the instrument is also well made. I have never seen artistic soundholes in an otherwise inartistically constructed instrument, but I have often seen a good scroll attached to a wretchedly designed and ill-made body. Scrolls may be bought ready made, but soundholes cannot be bought, unless the front table be bought too. In these days of high speed and hard pressure, makers who are not scrupulous about preserving the individuality of their instruments, and who care nought for the acclamation of posterity, frequently fix to their own make trunks, heads and necks that are of foreign workmanship. Of course, such mongrel productions as these instruments are do not deserve to be described as works of art. No great work of art has ever been created which is not the work of the artist himself from first to last, that is,

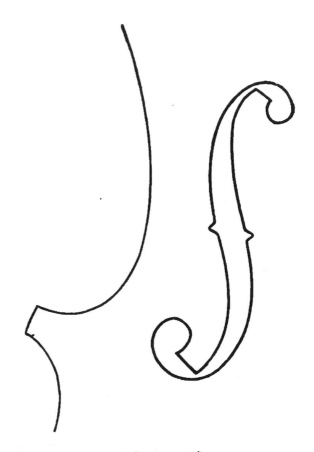

Soundhole of "Elephanta"
fecit in London, anno, 1899. Fig 4.

of course, excepting the mere accessories of the instrument, which are not essential to its being, but only to its *well*-being, as the Schoolmen would put it. The old masters made their own fingerboards, tail pieces, bridges, pegs—all except the strings, and there never have been such fine accessories made since.

Chapter 7.

WRITING " VIOLIN MAKING."

TOWARDS the end of the year 1899 Mayson was commissioned to write a series of articles for "The Strad," on the art of Violin Making. As it is not improbable that exception may be taken to certain remarks in this chapter, it is better that the main facts relative to this commission should be given *verbatim* in Mr. Mayson's own words. Here they are :—

"One day Mr. Lavender called on me in London," Mr. Mayson writes, "and asked if I would write the book referred to [i.e., "Violin Making"], much to my surprise, as, although I felt competent to undertake the work, I thought and said that there were others living who were more qualified than I for so difficult a task. Mr. Lavender was decidedly of another opinion; so, at my suggestion, the matter was left for my consideration.

.In the meantime I carefully weighed the proposal, putting the difficulties in one end of the scale, and

the by-no-means-liberal remuneration of five shillings
per column for such letterpress as I supplied copy
for, plus twopence per copy royalty on the book when
it should be reprinted, in the other end of the scale.
Poverty prevailed, and I accepted the commission. I
say 'poverty' advisedly, for *selling* violins is a very
different thing from making them. I accepted Mr.
Lavender's terms, with the verbal understanding that
all plates of photos and other illustrations should
count as 'copy.' Before I left London I made a
rough sketch of a plan on which I should proceed
with the work. You will gather the nature of my
modus operandi from a letter which appeared in
'The Strad' for July, 1902, on the subject.

When I returned to Manchester at the end of
1899, I set to work with a will on this work which,
I am told, will bring me fame—certainly not cash!
My experience of publishers and publishing reminds
me of what I once heard the late Mr. Ruskin—whom
I am proud to say I knew personally—say, when he
was asked why he was his own publisher. 'In every
flock there are a few black sheep, but in the flock of
publishers there are few white ones,' was the caustic
reply. Although, as I have every reason to believe,
my book has sold well, I have received not a cent
or a fraction thereof by way of royalty. People have
written me from near and far to say how pleased
they are with the work, and I have seen copies here
and there in different libraries, private and public,
with my own eyes—but I have received no royalty.

Publishers, my dear sir, are parasites that thrive on the mental system—ravens that live by picking the brains of helpless authors! Avoid them, as you would the evil one, if you can help it; or if yon cannot, and you have a strong attack of *cacoethes scribendi*, then cultivate friendship with the worms.

I spent no end of time in preparing and arranging my material, and a good deal of money on photographs for facsimile reproduction, so that when I came to cast up a profit and loss account I discovered that I was out of pocket on the venture. On the merits of the work I dare not speak: it is in the hands of the public, and public opinion must be my judge. All I wish to say is that it is the honest outcome of original thought, and I am prepared to let it stand or fall on its own merits."

It does not fall within the scope of this little work to express an opinion on the literary and technical merits of " Violin Making," suffice it to say that in the opinion of a number ot well-known experts the work is the best of its kind. As may be gathered from the foregoing remarks, the original articles were republished in book form in " The Strad Library "— a useful series of works on different subjects relating to the violin. Mr. Mayson wrote several things besides, such as " The Stolen Fiddle," " The Heir of Dalton," " Colazzi," " Poems and Dramas," all of which have been published; and " The Mystery of Windermere," " Minor Poems," etc., which are in manuscript.

Chapter 8.

The Third Period.

MR. MAYSON entered upon what may be conveniently described as his third period of violin making in 1900. From this time till the end of the year 1904, when he exchanged the earthly fiddle for the heavenly harp, there is observable a certain growth of art ideas which it is easier to feel than to describe. There is no departure from any previously established principle, or any sudden break in the train of thought, but merely growth of a more marked character, bearing a deeper impress of certain influences. The instruments of this period are characterized as much for excellency of finish as they are for originality of conception. During the years 1901—3 the artist received letters from all parts of the country expressive of delight at the manner in which he handled the subject of "Violin Making" in "The Strad," as well as a number of pressing invitations from well-to-do amateur makers to come and spend a short holiday with them. The consciousness of duty well-performed, coupled with these tokens of appreciation, wrought a miracle on the drooping spirits of the artist. Like Michael Angelo, he has recorded in verse how " these words of praise renovated and raised him who was almost numbered with the dead." The strongest plant grows etiolated for the lack of a little sunshine, and the sweetest flower fragrantless without the necessary moisture. Thus had Mayson been nearly " overcome as if bereft of reason," but now the sun of approval burst through the cloud of human apathy, and the cloud itself dispersed in a gentle shower of prosperity. The artist simply revelled in a new wealth of ideas, which he transferred into the blocks of wood which took shape in his hands with marvellous swiftness and felicity.

The latest work of Mayson has been judged by some connoisseurs to be inferior to that of his second period. The question of the relative merit of the work of the two periods is, perhaps, a somewhat idle one, but a word or two on the general idea involved may not be out of place here. The writer will not commit himself to an opinion one way or the other, but would deplore the ignorance which obtains as to the two conditions, which are of prime necessity in the sane estimation of any work of art. These are : an æsthetic training, and a true appreciation of the artist's object. For, as a recent writer has well-observed, " the perception of beauty does not come by nature. It is even more difficult than the perception of goodness or of truth. The eye requires education, as much as the voice, in order to attain high excellence : the eye, or rather that æsthetic sense of which the eye is the organ; and the higher the art is, the higher the education required to understand it. "This grand style," observes Sir Joshua Reynolds, "is artificial in the highest degree; it pre-supposes in the spectator a cultivated and prepared artificial state of the mind." But it is certain that in our days of incontinence of words, the great majority of those who favour the world with art criticisms possess no such cultivation. Superficial observers, they see superficial faults, or what they imagine to be faults. The high powers beneath escape them. Nor, apart from the matter of æsthetic cultivation, can it be admitted that the claim of very small men to judge summarily of very great ones, carries with it its own sanction. The works of an illustrious master are to be approached, not indeed in the spirit of blind and indiscriminate admiration, not with an abiding readiness to "wonder with a foolish face of praise"; but, surely, with diffidence, with modesty, with a feeling that, at all events, the presumption is in favour of the master being in the right. Again, the object which the artist had in view ought to be carefully ascertained and kept in mind. Ruskin, in a passage worthy of being deeply pondered (he uses the words, indeed, in another connection), divides artistes as searchers after truth into three classes: the first taking the good, and leaving the evil, the last perceiving evil only, while "the second or greatest class render all that they see * * * * unhesitatingy, with a kind of divine grasp and government of the whole: sympathising with all the good, and yet con-

"IVY," FECIT 1901.

"EVELINE," FECIT 1902.

fessing, permitting, and bringing the good out of, the evil also.''

Whatever cur opinions respecting the later art ideals of Mayson may be, it certainly behoves us to be lovers of truth and to admit at once that Mayson's ideals were characterized by sincere and absolute veracity.

In his carved back instruments he looks straight into the face of Nature for inspiration. He read Nature as a book, and he read to understand. As he read, so he depicted—not in the manner of another man, but in a style which he had dared to make peculiarly his own. He made many carved-back instruments during the last period. The secret of that which appeared to many devotees of the instrument a sheer waste of time and energy is this : the artist was impelled by his strong sense of the beautiful to express under the sensible material form and colour of wood and varnish the *hidden spiritual nature* of matter. In the sensible world around him Mayson found two elements diverse and distinct from each other, the idea and the form, spirit and matter, the invisible and the visible. In his carvings he sought to unite these two elements in such a way that each is expressed or manifested in the other—so that the form expressed the idea, the body the spirit, and the visible manifested the invisible. He sought to give expression to the spiritual principle which is the life and soul of things in sensible forms which the eye could see and the mind worship as it contemplated their lines.

Mr. Mayson was a firm believer in the reality of the invisible world. He believed further that there was a very real but mysterious bond between the seen and the unseen, and that the former was largely controlled by the latter. The writer once asked him if he were a spiritualist, and he replied in the negative, but said that he agreed with Professors Stewart and Tait, who say that " there exists now an invisible order of things intimately connected with the present, and capable of acting energetically upon it—for, in truth, the energy of the present system is to be looked upon as originally derived from the invisible universe, while the forces which give rise to transmutations of energy probably take their origin in the same region." Those who may happen to possess any of Mayson's lengthy epistles will know that he could spin out learned quotations of the above description *ad libitum*. He knew lengthy passages of Ruskin off by heart, and would often recite them aloud, waxing eloquent in their delivery, and becoming oblivious to his surroundings. He was a man of simple and earnest faith. Nothing could shake his belief in the efficacy of prayer. He was no great believer, however, in the necessity of any set form of prayer or praise, although an adherent of the Established Church, but preferred a species of mystical prayer—a sort of still communion with the Father of Spirits which transcends the imperfect offices of expressed praise or prayer. To exercise

"THIRD ANEMONE," FECIT 1902.

"MEREDITH MORRIS," VIOLIN,
FECIT 1903.

" Meredith Morris," Violin, fecit 1903.

faith meant to him to listen to the voices within the veil. "By communion with God," he wrote, quoting somebody, "I mean an utter losing of myself in Him, an entire self-abnegation, the lofty exaltation of which affords an atmosphere too rare for common mortals, and surrounds them with a temperature where even the breath of ordinary piety would freeze into icy vapour." The reader will not be surprised to learn that a man of this stamp attributed his growth in art to his growth in grace. The cynic may laugh the idea to scorn, but it was the honest conviction of our artist. In one of his letters he writes, "I shall not make the ideal fiddle till I live the ideal life." No doubt most of my readers will be inclined to say that in this no less than in other respects Mayson was far too serious a student of Ruskin. To those, however, who believe that the good, the true, and the beautiful are indissolubly united in the same immutable principle, Mayson will not appear as irrational as his critics. In June, 1903, he wrote, "I have now brought the real as near the borderland of the ideal as I dare hope to. Thanks to my struggles and disappointments, I have been able to sell the present for a pottage of lentiles. What we call the tangible is merely an evanescent vapour, that is, unless it has received the sign of immortality at the hands of the great Archetype. The Creed which is implied in these words will explain to you the development which you remark in my work. I am conscious of the change which has come over me. You would no doubt wish to know

the cause; here it is,—I have been BORN AGAIN. If
I continue to lead the simple life, I may yet live
to found a new school in violin making."

Mayson lived just eighteen months after writing
these words, and did not found a new school. Found
a new school! Poor man, could he have been so
utterly ignorant of the character of his English brethren
as to suppose that it were possible to found a school?
If he had been able to exert an influence anywhere
on aspirants to gouge and calipers honours, it would
have been at Manchester. But Mayson was the best
hated man in Manchester, which is the same as saying
that he was the greatest of its *luthier* prophets.
Jealousy begotten of rivalry in the domain of art
would appear to be a plant that is indigenous to
British soil. It is tolerably certain that the old
Cremonese did not partake of its deadly juice. The
great violin shops—the greatest the world has
ever seen—of Cremona were in close proximity to one
another in the Piazza S. Domenico, and there worked
the immortal *maestros*, almost cheek by jowl, in
perfect amity and undisturbed affability. Unfriendly
rivalry, we repeat, is characteristic of our nation, and,
in the sphere of art especially, it is the Nessus robe
which shrivels the life of high ideals. In one of our
English minsters is a beautiful window of vari-coloured
glass, which was made by a young apprentice out of
the bits of glass that had been rejected by his master;
and so far superior was it to all the other windows,
that the jealous artist killed himself with vexation.

The story is typical of a thousand more that might be cited in support of the above contention. Thanks to the orderings of a kind Providence, the last four years of Mayson's life were fringed with the silver of a little human kindness. Their story is pieced together in the following paragraphs from a number of letters which are now before me.

"One day," he writes (in 1903), "I received, at a moment when business was very depressed, a letter from a well-known M.D. of West Norwood, London, inviting me up to town with three of my best examples of violins, one of which he pledged himself to purchase. I went up, and was most kindly invited to become his guest for a day or two. On arriving at his residence, I found him living in good style, with a large practice, a handsome and amiable wife, and one baby boy. Mutual love of the fiddle at once begat friendly intercourse, and my violins so pleased him that we came to business at once. He purchased "Elephanta" and another instrument, and ordered four more violins to be specially made for him. This latter order was duly executed a few months later. One of the special instruments was the 'Harry Lavender,' the making of which is described in minute detail in 'Violin Making.' With regard to this second order, the arrangement between me and the doctor was to deliver the instruments by such and such a time, and to take a 'Pressenda' violin in part payment thereof, for which I was to allow £50. I regretted the bargain as far as the 'Italian' was concerned, for he had a cracked

voice, and I was glad to get rid of him at £20.
* * * Soon after this I received a pressing invitation
from a tried friend of mine at Bristol (whose young
son, a promising violinist, has two of my make of
violins) to run down for a day or two, as he wished
particularly to introduce to me a highly gifted young
lady violinist, aged about 15. Well, in my day, I
have had the honour of being asked for my opinion
many and many a time, respecting the merits of
youthful violinists, but I never expected to live to
hear anything so surpassingly beautiful from so young
a performer. The young lady arrived at the residence
of my friend, being escorted by her father. She was
rather a tall girl for her age, slim, graceful, and, I
feared, delicate. The moment she took her fiddle from
its case, and gave the strings a few preliminary
twangs, I knew I was in the presence of a genius,
and a short, fiery prelude, *apropos* of nothing in
particular to follow, so enraptured me that I was
quite lost to my environments. My friend told me
it was as great a treat for him to see my amazement
as it was to hear the young lady play. Truly, the
girl who stood before me, and who could set my
mind back at express pace to forgotten Paganinis
and Spohrs, was already a *virtuoso*. Her remarkable
execution, fine phrasing, intelligent rendering of
passages of great individuality,—her superb mastery of
the bow, whether in the delicate manipulation of
adagio or the abandon of *allegretto,* or in the power
and grip of the chords of Bach's *Chaconne*—hypnotized
the small, select audience. The name of this young

lady is now on everybody's lips—Marie Hall! She and
her clever father (to whom she owed her tuition up to
this time) engaged in animated conversation with me on
the most interesting of all topics—violin construction.
They greatly admired my work, and promised, when next
in Manchester, to call on me at my workshop. Well,
here is September, 1903, and Marie Hall is due to
play in October at that most exclusive of gatherings, the
Gentlemen's Concert. I wonder if my workshop will
see her. * * * Shortly after my visit to Bristol,
I spent a few days at Largs, West of Scotland. A
gentleman amateur, a reader of my 'Violin Making,'
invited me up to spend a few days with him, with
the object of giving him a few practical lessons in
violin construction. I gladly accepted his invitation,
and went. He met me at the Largs station, and
after a delightful walk up a long, wooded hill, running
parallel with the sea, arrived at his mansion, where I
was kindly received by my hostess. The mornings of
the following three days were devoted to setting the
amateur right in certain knotty points. I found him
to be very clever in the manipulation of tools, and
all the difficulties were therefore quickly overcome. In
the afternoons, he most kindly took me to see the
famous sights of the district—we went by steamer to
Rothsay, Bute, Oban, Arran, &c., and I accompanied
himself and another guest one day on a shooting
excursion. In the evenings we had music, and I was
charmed with the manner in which he played some
of the more celebrated strathspeys of his country. The
view from the front of the mansion was the most

.truly wonderful I have ever seen. Such an uninterrupted glory of scenery burst in on the eye that I was struck dumb with wonder, and had to lie down with sheer fatigue on the lawn under its weight. I realized then for the first time the meaning of that phrase—'the weight of glory.' Right before me stretched out the Firth of Clyde, with its innumerable islands in near, middle, and far distance. Beyond were the grand, noble lines of the mountains of Arran, which for grace and sublimity I have never seen equalled. There was, withal, a weirdness, a mysterious something about its mighty mass which was terribly impressive; for the sun-tipped peaks, with little of solidarity below, seemed suspended in mid-air, rising as they did like phantom ships from the ocean of morning mist which covered their base. * * * * Next autumn, correspondence again led to a visit,—this time to a schoolmaster, near Penrith, just under the Penine range, Of course, it was the old story—Would I go over and help in the early stages of the construction of an instrument? The schoolmaster referred to had my book, but he wanted oracular demonstration. He had it, and I found him clever as a wood carver, and very painstaking with detail work, and I had the satisfaction of seeing him well on the road before I left him. This gentleman paid me very marked attention, and he purchased one of my £30 instruments as a token of appreciation of the help I had given him. It was whilst here that I saw the finest made and best kept road in Great Britain. This was none other than the road constructed by the celebrated

McAdam for the Northern Mail, which to this day is the marvel of all the world. To see how breasts of hills were rounded, and how gently the curves were softened off—water never having the least chance to lodge, save in well-fashioned and perfectly-kept gutters and culverts—was, indeed, an object lesson in practical engineering, and a pleasurable surprise when I thought of the slovenly, slushy lanes of the country around Manchester. The authorities are proud, and justly so, of this road, and never is a loose stone or shovel-ful of earth allowed to disfigure its almost immaculate surface. From the schoolmaster's house I obtained a grand view of the far-away mountains around Keswick, and one evening I saw a sight that would baffle the poet's pen to describe, or the painter's brush to depict. A terrific storm of wind and rain swept across the fell in mid-distance, whereas the foreground as well as the lofty mountains beyond were bathed in brilliant sunshine. It lasted only about ten minutes, but its weird glory is treasure enough for a life-time. Shall I ever forget the awe which possessed me as I looked at the huge grey demon tearing down the fell, snorting as a battle stead, distorting perspective where he trampled, and throwing distances into utter confusion?

* * * * * * * *

I had a very agreeable surprise the other day. One Mr. Metcalfe, a watchmaker, of Newcastle-on-Tyne, wrote me that he had made three violins by the sole help of my book, although he was absolutely ignorant of the art before. He wished to be allowed to come and show them to me, which wish I gratified, of course. There was unmistakable talent in his work. He had done me the honour of naming the three instruments after each of my christian names and surname, and he had carved the word 'Mayson' on the back of the last one admirably, with other embellishments. He had failed in the varnish; but in this I shall help him, and with a few touches here and there, shall rectify the fault. I expect to find this gentleman very shortly turning out excellent work. * * * * I forgot to tell you that Sir William Ingram, Bart., wrote me from Kent in September of the present year (1903) to say that a well-known Professor in Australia had commissioned him to purchase a high-class modern violin for presentation out there. He said that he (Sir William) had read my 'Violin Making' with much pleasure, and was therefore led to ask me to make him a special instrument for transmission abroad. I executed the order at once, inasmuch as I had by me, completed, a magnificent violin named 'Ostera,' fecit 1899, which I was not ashamed to despatch to any part of the world, or see put in the hands of any *virtuoso* whatsoever. Sir William was delighted with the instrument. Among other things, he said—'You have most certainly solved that vexed question of tone.' This is no small praise from a man of Sir William Ingram's culture and tastes."

*   *   *   *

It is some consolation to think that the poor artist's last years were spent in comparative ease and comfort. The visits to different parts of the country, as well as the numerous letters of appreciation which he received, brought cheer and brightness to his home, inasmuch as they softened the lines of care on that venerable face which was its sun. The tranquility of the home is abundantly reflected in the sweet, delicate curves of the instruments of this period. Look at the accompanying illustrations of typical examples of the work of the years 1901-3. In one example especially, named "Third Anemone," simplicity and gracefulness of outline have assuredly reached the acme of perfection. Referring to the bas-relief on the back, an eminent painter and art critic remarked to me that if Mayson had been a painter or a sculptor instead of a violin maker, he would without a doubt have been one of the leading R.A.'s of modern times. The relief is from a drawing which had been specially made for the artist-craftsman by his friend and artist-author, Mr. John Ruskin. To get some idea of Mayson's mastery of form and proportion, it is only necessary to study the soundholes which are reproduced here.

Soundhole of "King Edward VII," fecit 1901.
(Violoncello) Fig.5.

The lines of this soundhole are bold, dignified, and withal tranquil. Still more characteristic are the lines of the soundhole, fig. 6. Here, we cannot but be struck with the versatility of the maker. No two pairs of soundholes are ever exactly alike. The

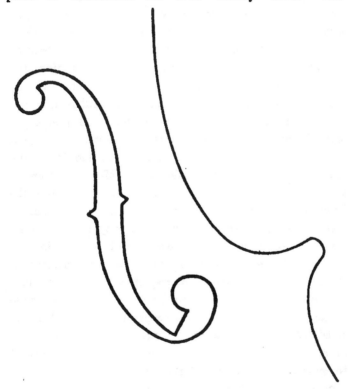

Soundhole, 1901, Fig. 6.

trained eye will discover minute differences of size, form, inclination, and position in the *f*'s of all the

instruments of the third period. Some are a fraction
longer and narrower than others, whereas the angle of
inclination increases or lessens variously, according to
the general contour of the instrument. The sweep of
the upper and lower curves of the soundhole under
consideration extends to nearly the centre-notches. The
balance between the upper and lower portions is faultless.
With regard to the inclination, it is to be observed
specially that Mayson's principle of determining the
angle was based on the doctrine of equilibrium. If you
cut any one of his soundholes out in a cardboard, taking
care to be very exact with the outline, and pass a pin
through midway between the centre-notches, the f will
assume a certain position in equilibrium, due to gravit-
ation. This is the angle adopted by Mayson. Here is
another characteristic soundhole, fig. 7. This gives the
impression of being shorter than the former, but is
really of exactly the same length, as may be ascertained
from measurement. The width differs, as do the
curves, and the difference accounts for the increase in
the angle of inclination in respect to the longitudinal
axis of the fiddle, in accordance with the principle
already stated. It is not suggested here that the
artist determined the angle of inclination experimentally
in each case. It were as unnecessary as it were absurd
to suppose such a procedure. It is the property of
genius to be able to do intuitively what science
determines to be correct experimentally. Stradivari
did not harmonize the densities of his back and front
tables by the help of the hydrostatic balance: his
scholastic attainments barely carried him far enough

to cast his accounts in proper form. He was guided by the senses of sight and touch, and by that subtle something—a sort of sixth sense—which has not yet received a proper name. It is even doubtful whether he used mechanical calipers—the probability is that his own long fingers served him in better stead.

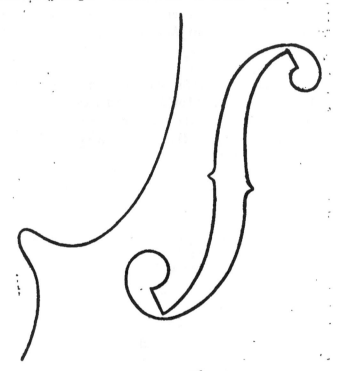

Soundhole, 1902, Fig. 7.

It is remarkable to what degree of perfection the sense of touch can be developed. Sir William Hamilton observes that a blind man of his acquaintance could tell the colour of a fowl's feathers by stroking them. Modern science declares that the finger tips of blind people, from long practice with the Brille type, acquire new nerve cells charged with the same kind of grey nerve matter as the brain. If modern makers relied less on mechanical contrivances and more on their own intuitive powers, modern Art would have less to be ashamed of than it has.

Here is another beautiful soundhole, fig. 8; it belongs to the last instrument but four made by the artist. The contemplation of the melting curves of this *f* almost converts one to Hogarth's doctrine of the line of beauty.

The dimensions adopted by Mayson for his later violins are:

Length of body	$14\frac{5}{16}$	inches.
Width across upper bouts ..	$6\frac{7}{8}$	,,
,, ,, middle bouts ..	$4\frac{1}{2}$	,,
,, ,, lower bouts ..	$8\frac{1}{2}$	,,
Depth of rib at lower bouts	$1\frac{1}{4}$	,,
,, ,, upper bouts	$1\frac{1}{8}$	,,
Length of soundholes (usual)	3	,,
Distance between soundholes at upper turn (usual) ·..	$1\frac{5}{8}$	,,

The arching is slightly more pronounced than that adopted by Stradivari in his grand period. The varnish is Mayson's own composition, of various colours, ranging from pale, straw-coloured amber, to bright orange-red and deep brown: it is of a very elastic

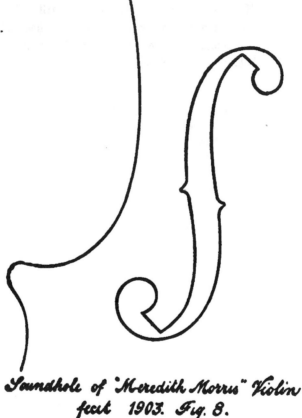

Soundhole of "Meredith Morris" Violin
fecit 1903. Fig. 8.

oil, perfectly transparent, and free from any thought of cracking. It was laid on in the manner described by the maker in his well-known work, "Violin Making," in from fifteen to twenty very thin coats, during the summer months. Mayson observed a hard and fast rule with regard to the season of varnishing. He never began varnishing till the thermometer registered 64 degrees of natural heat (Fah.) in the workshop, and he ceased to do so as soon as it fell below that mark again.

Chapter 9.

A Tardy Recognition.

AFTER long years of cold neglect on the part of the musical public in general, and of the . Manchester violin world in particular, the genius of Mayson was at length recognised in a public manner. A movement was organized for the purpose of raising funds to purchase a number of his best instruments, which were to be presented to the Royal Museums of Peel Park, Salford, and South Kensington, London. The Committee, consisting of. several prominent citizens of Manchester, and other admirers of the artist's work, appointed Mr. Alfred Shaw, of Southlands, Whalley Range, their secretary, and the Messrs. Forsyth Brothers, Ltd., of Deansgate, treasurers. The Manchester press took the matter up, and letters were published in the columns of the "Guardian" and the "Evening Chronicle" relative to the movement. The "Chronicle" sent a special correspondent to interview Mayson, and a lengthy article (illustrated with views of three different instruments) appreciatory of his life and work appeared in its columns.

I cannot do better than reproduce here the article named, together with one of a series of letters which were published in the "Manchester Guardian" on the same subject. It is better to allow these witnesses to truth and worth to give evidence in their own words than to give any mere paraphrase or epitome of what they say.

From the *Manchester Evening Chronicle*:

A MANCHESTER VIOLIN MAKER:
MAKING MUSIC FOR POSTERITY.

The electric cars running along Oxford Street, soon after dipping under the railway bridge near Oxford Road Station, pass a row of tall upright houses on the right hand side, with shops beneath them. There is nothing at all about the formal fronts to call special attention to them. The shop windows, splashed with mud from the passing traffic, and covered with sooty moisture distilled from the near vomiting chimneys, are full of an uninviting miscellany. Globes and burners for incandescent gaslights; ready-made garments of drab colours, picture postcards and cheap stationery, compete dully for interest with a pork butcher's, and a shop where they sell the "Police News," and a cheap confectioner's. As the rain pours down and the hurrying foot passengers hide themselves beneath sombre umbrellas, one is grateful for the little touch of brightness that comes from the pile of oranges in the window across the street. Even when the sun shines there can be little colour, except what the new paint of the gliding cars brings with it, in this commonplace thoroughfare. Once a pleasant road, with fields beyond, suburbia now leaves it far behind, and the only object of the well dressed people in the cars is to get out as soon as possible. It might seem odd, then, if I asked you to get off the car and stop at one of these uninteresting shop windows. It is full of violins and other musical instruments; you might find a dozen like it within half-a-mile of the centre of the town. What would be the thoughts of the Manchester citizen of to-day if he could be told perchance two hundred years hence this shop, and a certain small room above it, would be known to foreigners as the church at Stratford-on-Avon is, or the Burns cottage on the banks of the Doon, or the mound that marks the sight of Fotheringhay Castle?

Prophecies that take two centuries to fulfil are easy to make; whether there is a possibility of this particular one coming true must be judged by those who read the rest of this article.

I said the shop was like a dozen others in Manchester. It is, so far as external appearances go. If you know something about violins you will not say so when you have spent a few minutes inside. If you have any eye at all for the form of a violin—colour, grain, and contour, as well as general design—your interest will be quickly aroused. In a small workroom at the top of the house there hangs, amid much litter of violins made and in the making, an instrument which may some day be historic. It is the first fiddle ever made by Walter H. Mayson, who has worked in this room for more than twelve years. It is not a perfect instrument, any more than "Pauline" is a perfect poem. Yet it may have an interest for posterity greater than that which attaches to the lovely creation

of fine-grained wood whose rich varnish you now see
drying on the line above your head.

Do you recollect that passage in the "Autocrat" in
which the author discusses some of the things whose
value consists in that they have been kept and used?
The old Violin is one of them, and the genial "Autocrat"
sketches in thought its forgotten story—played on by
ancient maestros, by the young enthusiast in his hidden
love, by the cold virtuoso, by the lonely prisoner and the
improvident artist, by the humble convent-dweller and the
careless reveller, by the gentle dilettante, who makes it
answer him softly, as it did the old maestros—until at
last it is given into our hands, "its pores full of
music, stained like the meerschaum, through and through,
with the concentrated hue and sweetness of all the
harmonies which have kindled and faded on its strings."
It is in the hope of some such future as this for his
handiwork that Mr. Mayson has toiled for a quarter
of a century at an obscure and ill-remunerated task. He
is making music for posterity, and he is content in the
thought that posterity will appreciate his labours.
There is now an opportunity for his own generation
to do so. A project for purchasing two of Mr. Mayson's
finest carved instruments for presentation to Peel Park
and South Kensington Museums opens a way for the
recognition by the Manchester musicians, tardy though
it be, of the genius of one of their townsmen, while
it is my excuse for calling attention to his work. Mr.
Mayson began making fiddles when he was thirty nine
years old. The first child of his brain—and equally
of his hand and eye—is the instrument we saw just
now in that upper room. He made it at "The Polygon,"
Lower Broughton, beginning it on October 16, 1873.
Like most other artists, Mayson had plenty of difficulties
to struggle against at the outset of his career. He

showed a schoolboy talent for the skilful use of tools,
and made some Aeolian harps, with an ingenious contrivance for quadrupling their sound. But his parents
apprenticed him to a commercial firm in Manchester.
Poetry and other literary work engaged his leisure,
and he was thirty-nine when he made his first violin.
It had not the quality of a Cremona, but it was thought
so well of by some of those capable of judging that
he was advised to persevere. Two years later he felt
himself strong enough to throw up his business appoint-
ment, and to set himself with his whole energies to
the art which he has since pursued. His first workshop was at Barton Arcade; then he went to Croft
House, Newby Bridge, at the foot of Windermere; and
six years afterwards he removed to the strangely different
surroundings at 62 Oxford Road, where we have found
him this rainy morning. Mr. Mayson has close ties with
the Lake district. He was born in 1835 at Cheetwood,
Manchester, but his father was a Keswickian, and his
mother was the daughter of William Green, the friend
of the Lake poets and the recorder of their haunts.

It is time to say something about the instruments to
which Mr. Mayson has given his life. He has made
nearly 750 violins, violas, and violoncellos, and hopes
to make many more.

The first thing to notice is that he is entirely self-
taught, and the second that every portion of his
violins is his unaided work.

" How, then, is it possible that an untaught English-
man, with no hereditary faculty and no traditional
experience such as guides the hand of the Italian
fiddle-maker of his day, can have found the way to

fashion instruments comparable with the best work of Cremonese school? It is his enthusiasm and indomitable courage, added to extraordinary skill of hand and eye, that have enabled him to combat the difficulties that beset him and to make each fiddle more perfect than the last.

It may seem an extraordinary claim that his work is worthy to be mentioned beside that of men whose names are immortal in this art. The claim, however, has been made by some who are qualified to judge. The measure of success which his unwearying enthusiasm has achieved may be seen in the testimony of the Rev. W. Meredith Morris, author of "Violin-Makers of To-day." Mr. Meredith Morris boldly avers that his "Cordelia," made by Mr. Mayson, is "The queen of all fiddles which I have ever seen." He has examined, he says, nearly a thousand fiddles of modern make during the last three years. "About one-third of these were high-class, and some really fine instruments, but not one of them will touch 'Cordelia.' She is not of a class—she is 'sui generis.' To say that the mantle of Stradivari has fallen upon you is not enough. If I believed in transmigration, I should say that you were Stradivari, and that you had learned a great deal during the various stages of your migration." The same gentleman becomes, if possible, even more enthusiastic over his "Cordelia" in an article in "The Strad." A grander fiddle than "Cordelia," he declares, "never has been, never can be made," and he believes that fiddles of this class will worthily replace the "*chefs d'œuvre*" of Cremona when the latter become food for worms. Another eminent critic has declared that Mr. Mayson "Has accomplished that which not one in ten thousand has courage even to attempt, and that is, that he has given us straight from the workshop a tone

such as it has been contended for a hundred and fifty
years could not be produced, and which it would take
a hundred years to create by incessant labour from a
modern violin. Perhaps the most famous violin which has
come from the unpretentious workshop is the one known as
the " Hallé-Mayson." It was constructed in memory
of Sir Charles Hallé, and is declared by a writer in
the " Violin Times " to be " in every way a worthy
souvenir of the man in whose honour it has been made."
Of late years Mr. Mayson has added another art to his
accomplishments. Not content with an exquisite workmanship and such a perfection of grain and varnish as
are not to be found in any modern violins, he has
commenced to carve the backs of some of his instruments. The remarkable skill shown in the manipulation
of so thin and delicate a material can be seen only by an
inspection of his work.   *   *   *   *   Mr. Mayson
has recently been gratified by a notification of the fact
that one of his carved instruments will be accepted at
Peel Park Museum, and he is now at work on a fiddle
for this purpose. For conscientious workmanship, if his
work went no further than that, no smaller compliment
would be deserved. Only those who have seen the
fiddles in the making, and the elaborate pains that go
to every process, can realise how hardly the honours he
reaps are won. He has fought many years against
scant recognition. His townsfolk cannot make the memory
of the neglected years less bitter to him. They *can*
render his remaining ones happier in knowing that at
last a prophet has some honour in his own country.

The following letter, among others, appeared in the
columns of the " Guardian " :—

To the Editor of the " Manchester Guardian."

SIR,—In the deeply interesting article of a correspondent

in your issue of the 27th ult., following upon the
practical letter of Mr. H. C. Hughes on the 19th, the
people of Manchester were asked to show some timely
recognition of Mr. Walter H. Mayson's work in having
done more, probably, than any living man to raise the
standard of the cult of violin-making. Leaders in the
musical world in this city have expressed their deep
respect for the enthusiasm of his work and their
admiration of its success.

We are glad to have him in our midst to-day. It
may not be for long, for the hand grows weary and the
brain cannot outlast its best work. It is surely wise for
some among us at least to show by our generous action
now that we were not open to the charge that when
very high merit came to us we were too blind to see it
and too callous to the art we love to encourage it. A
committee, composed of gentlemen interested in Mayson's
work, has been formed with the object of placing on
permanent record their high appreciation of his zealous
devotion to the art of violin-making and the crowning
triumph of his success after a period of 30 years'
labour, and to accomplish this it is proposed to purchase
five of his best examples of plain and carved-back
fiddles for presentation to and exhibition in the South
Kensington and Owens College Museums, thereby
providing a lasting memorial of his work and genius.

The following gentlemen have kindly consented to
supplement the existing Committee : The Rev. Canon
Rawnsley, Mr. Charles Sutton, Mr. Wellesley Peel
Roberts, and Mr. E. Bucknall, of Bristol. The Committee will be glad to add to their number the names
of any ladies or gentlemen who sympathise with what
they believe to be an undertaking on behalf of a worthy

man who will be recognised in the future as having a claim to a place among Manchester's honoured citizens.

Subscriptions may be remitted to Messrs. Forsyth Brothers, Limited, Deansgate, Manchester.—I am, &c. (on behalf of the Committee),

ALFRED SHAW.

Southlands, Manley Road, Whalley Range,
Manchester, September 10, 1902.

Here was, at last, an honest effort to heal the wound caused by thirty years' neglect. If the labours of the Committee were not crowned with the success which they deserved, and which the worthiness of the object demanded, it was not their fault. The faithful services of Mr. Shaw, the energetic secretary, deserve to be specially mentioned, for without these the movement would have collapsed before a fraction of the necessary funds had been got together. The sum realized fell far short of the anticipated figure, and only one instrument could be purchased; this was a carved-back violin, named "Coronation," fecit in 1902. The instrument was offered to and accepted by the authorities of Peel Park Museum, where it is now deposited, and where it will rest as long as any portion of its anointed fabric remains to be seen.

Chapter 10.

The Passing of the Artist.

MR. MAYSON'S severe illness in London impaired his general health, and he was never free from slight but recurrent attacks of pain thereafter. He had a second attack towards the close of 1902, of a less acute nature but longer duration than the first. When he had recovered he wrote me about his illness as follows: "I was seized with a severe pain under the left shoulder, which I and the family physician considered to be rheumatic pain. But medical treatment seemed to accentuate rather than alleviate my pain, so I consulted Dr. Moore, of Miles Platting, who is a member of the congregation of S. Luke's Church there, where I also attend. He said at once that my heart was affected, and that I was in a serious condition. He said I was not to do any work for a time, or walk long distances. He attended me twice a week for several weeks, and gave me medicine to take. I am particular to state these facts, as I want to make known that no christian gentleman ever gave himself up to a good work more thoroughly than did this clever physician to the task of 'patching' me up. He has the satisfaction of now seeing me convalescent and able to do a little work again. I can never forget his kindness. He would take from me no payment whatever for his attendance or medicine —and the medicine, in all conscience, was enough in quantity to fill a surgery. It is some satisfaction to me to remember that I got him to accept two of William Green's (my grandfather), etchings of Ambleside."

On November 18th, 1904, Mr. Mayson had a slight paralytic seizure, from which he only partially rallied. On December 26th, he had a second stroke, and he never regained complete consciousness from then till his death, which took place on the last day of the year. He was buried on the following Wednesday, January 4th, 1905, in his father's grave, at S. Paul's, Kersal, near Manchester. The funeral was attended by relatives and family friends, and the ark containing the mortal remains of the immortal artist was covered with beautiful wreaths. The coffin bore the simple inscription : " Walter Henry Mayson ; died 31st December, 1904, aged 70 years."

An inexpensive stone stands at the head of the simple, grave, bearing the following inscription:

WALTER HENRY MAYSON,

VIOLIN MAKER,

WHO PASSED AWAY DEC. 31ST, 1904,

AGED 70 YEARS.

"A WORKMAN THAT NEEDETH NOT TO BE ASHAMED."

"I HAVE GLORIFIED THEE ON EARTH . . . I HAVE FINISHED THE WORK THOU GAVEST ME TO DO."

Appendices.

Appendix A.

REGISTER OF VIOLINS, VIOLAS, AND VIOLONCELLOS
MADE BY WALTER HENRY MAYSON.

No.	Date on which completed in the white.	Description.	Name.
1	Oct. 16, 1873 ...	Violin	...
2	Jan. 1, 1874 ...	,,	...
3	Feb. 5 ,, ...	,,	...
4	Mar. 4 ,, ...	,,	...
5	April 1 ,, ...	,,	...
6	,, 27 ,, ...	Viola	...
7	May 20 ,, ...	Violin	...
8	June 15 ,, ...	,,	...
9	,, 27 ,, ...	,,	...
10	July 16 ,, ...	,,	...
11	Aug. 6 ,, ...	,,	...
12	,, 21 ,, ...	,,	...
13	Sept. 3 ,, ...	,,	...
14	,, 7 ,, ...	,,	...
15	Oct. 2 ,, ...	,,	...
16	,, 22 ,, ...	Viola	...
17	Nov. 8 ,, ...	Violin	...

No.	Date on which completed in the white.		Description.		Name.
18	Nov. 20, 1874	...	Violin	...	
19	Dec. 1	,, ...	,,	...	
20	,, 9	,, ...	,,	...	
21	,, 24	,, ...	,,	...	
22	Jan. 12, 1875	...	,,	...	
23	,, 25	,, ...	,,	...	
24	Feb. 11	,, ...	,,	...	
25	Mar. 12	,, ...	,,	...	
26	,, 28	,, ...	,,	...	
27	April 20	,, ...	,,	...	
28	June 1	,, ...	,,	...	
29	,, 11	,, ...	,,	...	
30	,, 25	,, ...	,,	...	
31	July 13	,, ...	,,	...	
32	Aug. 18	,, ...	,,	...	
33	,, 30	,, ...	,,	...	
34	Sept. 18	,, ...	,,	...	
35	,, 30	,, ...	,,	...	
36	Oct. 15	,, ...	,,	...	
37	Nov. 8	,, ...	,,	...	
38	,, 29	,, ...	,,	...	
39	Dec. 13	,, ...	,,	...	
40	,, 29	,, ...	,,	...	
41	Jan. 19, 1876	...	,,	...	
42	Feb. 7	,, ...	,,	...	
43	,, 25	,, ...	,,	...	
44	March 5	,, ...	,,	...	
45	,, 16	,, ...	,,	...	
46	,, 28	,, ...	,,	...	Madam

No.	Date on which completed in the white.	Description.	Name.
47	April 7, 1876	... Violin	... Mit Tweeto
48	,, 28 ,,	... ,,	... Amelia
49	May 15 ,,	... ,, :	... Anymone
50	June 1 ,,	... ,,	...
51	July 1 ,,	... ,,	...
52	,, 13 ,,	... ,,	... Sarah
53	,, 25 ,,	... ,,	... Spohr
54	Aug. 8 ,,	... ,,	... E. M. Nunn
55	,, 22 ,,	... ,,	... Beethoven
56	Sept. 5 ,,	... ,,	... Mozart
57	,, 19 ,,	... ,,	... Schubert
58	Oct. 2 ,,	... ,,	... Wagner
59	,, 14 ,,	... ,,	... Don Pedro
60	,, 27 ,,	... ,,	... Holmes
61	Nov. 8 ,,	... ,,	... Colazzi
62	,, 25 ,,	... ,,	... Joachim
63	Dec. 13 ,,	... ,,	... Scarlet Fever
64	Jan. 8, 1877	... ,,	... Galileo
65	,, 26 ,,	... ,,	... Princess Royal
66	Feb. 10 ,,	... ,,	... Queen Victoria (No. 1)
67	,, 23 ,,	... ,,	... Friday
68	Mar. 13 ,,	... ,,	... Prince of Wales
69	,, 24 ,,	... ,,	... Bradbury
70	April 13 ,,	... ,,	... Pickering
71	,, 24 ,,	... ,,	... The Emperor
72	May 7 ,,	... ,,	... Wilhelmj
73	June 1 ,,	... Violoncello	.. The Strad
74	July 4 ,,	... ,,	... Amaranthus Maysonus

No,	Date on which completed in the white.		Description.	Name.
75	July	31, 1877 ...	Viola ...	A. M. Ruber
76	Aug.	14 ,, ...	Violoncello...	Abel of Manchester
77	Sept.	6 ,, ...	Violin ...	Ye Blokat
78	,,	19 ,, ...	,, ...	Bassop
79	,,	27 ,, ...	,, ...	Major Morgan
80	Oct.	6 ,, ...	,, ...	Atlas
81	,,	15 ,, ...	,, ...	A. Maysonus
82	,,	25 ,, ...	,, ...	Tictyreus
83	Nov.	5 ,, ...	,, ...	Guy Fawkes
84	,,	15 ,, ...	,, ...	Kars
85	,,	25 ,, ...	,, ...	Seaton
86	Dec.	6 ,, ...	,, ...	Plevna
87	,,	27 ,, ...	,, ...	Old 1877
88	Jan.	8, 1878 ...	,, ...	Young 1878
89	,,	26 ,, ...	,, ...	Alcestis
90	Feb.	6 ,, ...	,, ...	Victor Emanuel
91	,,	15 ,, ...	,, ...	Abominable Czar
92	,,	28 ,, ...	,, ...	Ye Traitor of '78
93	Mar.	11 ,, ...	,, ...	Lord Beaconsfield
94	,,	19 ,, ...	,, ...	Eurydice
95	,,	28 ,, ...	,, ...	Lord Derby
96	April	5 ,, ...	,, ...	San Stephano
97	,,	15 ,, ...	,, ...	Alcibiades
98	,,	26 ,, ...	,, ...	Amaranth
99	May	3 ,, ...	,, ...	Orpheus
100	,,	13 ,, ...	,, ...	No. One Hundred
101	,,	20 ,, ...	,, ...	Centurion
102	,,	28 ,, ...	,, ...	Alpha
103	June	7 ,, ...	,, ...	Autolychus

No.	Date on which completed in the white.			Description.	Name.
104	June	21, 1878	...	Violin	... The Dragon
105	July	3 ,,	...	,,	... Duchess of Edinboro'
106	,,	11 ,,	...	,,	... Duke of Edinboro'
107	,,	23 ,,	...	,,	... Berlin
108	Aug.	2 ,,	...	,,	... Abraham
109	,,	12 ,,	...	,, .	... Adelieda
110	,,	26 ,,	...	,,	... Dragonius
111	Sept.	3 ,,	...	,,	... Old River
112	,,	11 ,,	...	,,	... Ate
113	,,	19 ,,	...	,,	... The Ameer
114	,,	28 ,,	...	,,	... Queenstown
115	Oct.	7 ,,	...	,,	... Afghan
116	,,	17 ,,	...	,,	... Lord Nelson
117	Nov.	2 ,,	...	,,	... Florence
118	,,	8 ,,	...	,,	... Gualterus
119	,,	15 ,,	...	,,	... Ali Musjed
120	,,	28 ,,	...	,,	... Jellalabad
121	Dec.	7 ,,	...	,,	... Princess Alice (In Memoriam)
122	,,	23 ,,	...	,,	... Old 1878
123	Jan.	10, 1879	...	,,	... Young 1879
124	,,	23 ,,	...	,,	... Empress
125	,,	31 ,,	...	,,	... The Great
126	Feb.	14 ,,	...	,,	... St. Valentine
127	,,	24 ,,	...	,,	... Ida
128	Mar.	5 ,,	...	,,	... Boadicea
129	,,	18 ,,	...	,,	... The Gem
130	,,	29 ,,	...	Violoncello	... Joseph

No.	Date on which completed in the white.		Description.	Name.
131	April 21, 1879	...	Viola	... Alice Maud
132	May 5 ,,	...	Violin	... Autocrat
133	,, 13 ,,	...	,,	... Alma
134	,, 22 ,,	...	.,	... The Sun
135	,, 31 ,,	...	,,	... Kaiser
136	June 10 ,,	...	,,	... Prince Imperial
137	,, 30 ,,	...	Violoncello	... Pompey
138	July 15 ,,	...	Viola	... Pompey's Wife
139	,, 28 ,,	...	Violin	... Pompey's Son
140	Aug. 6 ,,	...	,,	... Pompey's Daughter (The Pompey Quartette.)
141	,, 18 ,,	...	Violin	... Old Clegg
142	,, 25 ,,	...	,,	...Frank (In Memoriam)
143	Sept. 5 ,,	...	,,	... Wintorius
144	,, 16 ,,	...	,,	... The Wonder
145	,, 25 ,,	...	,,	... Aurora
146	Oct. 5 ,,	...	,,	... W. Tattersall (In Memoriam)
147	,, 14 ,,	...	,, $\frac{3}{4}$ size	... My first Baby
148	,, 31 ,,	...	Viola	... Il Maestro
149	Nov. 11 ,,	...	Violin	... Pacific
150	,, 22 ,,	...	,,	... Napoleon III.
151	Dec. 1 ,,	...	,,	... Il Penseroso
152	,, 15 ,,	...	,,	... L' Allegro
153	,, 30 ,,	...	Viola	... In. Memoriam
154	Jan. 10, 1880	...	Violin	... The Lyre
155	,, 20 ,,	...	,,	... Leonarda da Vinci
156	Feb. 2 ,,	...	,, (carved back)	Rose Bonheur

No.	Date on which completed in the white.	Description.	Name.
157	April 17, 1880 ...	Violin	... Moliere
158	March 1 ,, ...	,,	... S. Mathew
159	,, 12 ,, ...	,,	... S. Mark
160	,, 20 ,, ...	,,	... S. Luke
161	,, 27 ,, ...	,,	... S. John
162	April 9 ,, ...	,,	... Jupiter
163	,, 20 ,, ...	,,	... Venus
164	May 1 ,, ...	,,	... Adonis
165	,, 15 ,, ...	,,	... Celeste
166	June 1 ,, ...	,,	... Ne Plus Ultra
167	,, 30 ,, ...	,,	... Theophiletus
168	July 8 ,, ...	,,	... Leonora
169	,, 16 ,, ...	,,	... Juno
170	,, 25 ,, ...	,,	... Jove
171	Aug. 12 ,, ...	,,	... Cupid
172	,, 22 ,, ...	,,	... Nicholas Amati
173	Sept. 3 ,, ...	,, (scroll cut through)	The Devil
174	,, 14 ,, ...	,,	... The Angel
175	,, 24 ,, ...	,,	... Titus
176	Oct. 2 ,, ...	,,	... Dulcigno
177	,, 15 ,, ...	Violoncello	... Ruskin
178	Nov. 8 ,, ...	Violin	... My Mother
179	,, 20 ,, ...	,,	... My Father
180	Dec. 4 ,, ...	,,	... Minesto
181	,, 11 ,, ...	,,	... Dunedin
182	,, 20 ,, ...	,,	... Carlyle
183	Jan. 1, 1881 ...	,, (carved back)	Anemone (No. 1)

No.	Date on which completed in the white.			Description.		Name.
184	Jan.	12, 1881	...	Violin	...	Experiment
185	,,	22	,,	...	,,	... The Success
186	Feb.	3	,,	...	,,	... Pompeii
187	,,	20	,,	...	,, (carved back & scroll)	Portinscale
188	March	1	,,	...	,,	... Scafell
189	April	3	,,	...	,,	... Tobolsk
190	May	5	,,	...	,,	... Desdemona
191	,,	20	,,	...	,, (sold in the white)	Othello
192	June	15	,,	...	,,	...
193	,,	21	,,	...	,,	...
194	,,	14	,,	...	,,	... Hamlet
195	,,	28	,,	...	,,	... Ophelia
196	July	5	,,	...	,,	... The Storm
197	,,	9	,,	...	,,	... Edmund Burke
198	,,	18	,,	...	,,	... Irene
199	,,	26	,,	...	,, ($\frac{3}{4}$ size)	Tommy
200	Aug.	2	,,	...	,,	... No. 200
201	,,	9	,,	...	,,	... Guinevere
202	,,	16	,,	...	,,	... Isoult
203	,,	25	,,	...	,,	... Lyncette
204	Sept.	1	,,	...	,,	... Elaine
205	,,	8	,,	...	,,	... Prometheus
206	,,	20	,,	...	Viola	... Garfield
207	,,	29	,,	...	Violin	... Ouida
208	Oct.	8	,,	...	,,	... Southey
209	,,	15	,,	...	,,	... Lady of the Lake

No.	Date on which completed in the white			Description.	Name.
210	Oct. 26, 1881	...		Violin	... Roderic Dhu
211	Nov. 8	,,	...	,,	... Lucretia
212	Dec. 3	,,	...	,,	... Agricola
213	,, 20	,,	...	,,	... Semapore
214	Jan. 1, 1882	...		,,	... Vixen
215	,, 24	,,	...	,,	... Violet
216	Feb. 1	,,	...	,,	... Sims Reeves
217	,, 14	,,	...	,,	... Helen
218	,, 22	,,	...	,,	... Sun Flower
219	March 6	,,	...	,,	... Jumbo
220	,, 15	,,	...	,,	... Heroine
221	April 2	,,	...	,,	... Folfarine
222	,, 12	,,	...	,, (carved back)	I will arise
223	,, 27	,,	...	,,	... Lord Frederick Cavendish
224	May 6	,,	...	,,	... T. H. Burke
225	,, 19	,,	...	,,	... Mancunium
226	Aug. 1	,,	...	Viola	... Braham
227	,, 12	,,	...	Violin	... Lord of the Isles
228	,, 22	,,	...	,,	... Hawkshead
229	Sept. 9	,,	...	,,	... Carrodus
230	,, 18	,,	...	,,	... Grace Darling
231	Oct. 4	,,	...	,,	... Valdivia
232	,, 14	,,	...	,,	... Marmion
233	,, 24	,,	...	,,	... Tancredi
234	Nov. 2	,,	...	,,	... Hungarian
235	,, 10	,,	...	,,	... The Original
236	,, 23	,,	...	,,	... Leonora (No. 2)

No.	Date on which completed in the white.			Description.	Name.
237	Dec.	4,	1882 ...	Violin	... Xantippe
238	,,	15	,, ...	,,	... Hercules
239	,,	28	,, ...	,,	... Hesperus
240	Jan.	10,	1883 ...	,,	... Spenser
241	,,	25	,, ...	,,	... Sarasate
242	Feb.	5	,, ...	,,	... Socrates
243	,,	14	,, ...	,,	... St. Valentine (No. 2)
244	,,	26	,, ...	,,	... Ideste Fideles
245	March	6	,, ...	,,	... Isolde
246	,,	15	,, ...	Violoncello...	Windermere Giant
247	,,	31	,, ...	Violin	... The Challenge
248	April	7	,, ...	,, ($\frac{3}{4}$ size)	
249	,,	25	,, ...	,,	... Paganini
250	May	7	,, ...	,,	... Rositha
251	,,	12	,, ...	,,	... Cove of Cork
252	,,	30	,, ...	,,	... Shakespeare
253	June	6	,, ...	,,	... Eskdale
254	,,	25	,, ...	,,	... Wastdale
255	July	9	,, ...	,,	... Mosedale
256	Aug.	8	,, ...	,,	... Ennerdale
257	,,	24	,, ...	,,	... Ambleside
258	Sept.	10	,, ...	,,	... The Monarch
259	,,	26	,, ...	Violoncello...	Lady Jane
260	Oct.	18	,, ...	Violin	... Leonora III
261	,,	30	,, ...	.,	... Fidelis
262	Nov.	16	,, ...	,,	... Corniston
263	Dec.	10	,, ...	,,	... Jewdale
264	,,	28	,, ...	,,	... Barrowdale
265	Jan.	11,	1884 ...	,,	... Lammermoor

No.	Date on which completed in the white.	Description.	Name.
266	Jan. 22, 1884 ...	Violin ...	Asuda
267	Feb. 7 ,, ...	,, ...	Silvia
268	,, 14 ,, ...	,, ...	Hermion
	(Private marks put in all instruments hereafter)		
269	Feb. 23, 1884 ...	Violin ...	Eamont
270	March 5 ,, ...	,, (carved back)	Anemone (No. 2)
271	,, 14 ,, ...	,, ...	Patterdale
272	,, 22 ,, ...	,, ...	Leopold
273	April 3 ,, ...	,, ...	The Glen
274	,, 14 ,, ...	,, ...	Blencathra
275	,, 23 ,, ...	Violoncello ...	Apollo
276	May 6 ,, ...	Violin ...	Little Nell
277	,, 12 ,, ...	,, ...	Fergus McIvor
278	,, 24 ,, ...	,, ...	Flora McIvor
279	June 12 ,, ...	,, ...	The Empress (No. 2)
280	,, 25 ,, ..	,, ...	Orpheus (No. 4)
281	July 3 ,, ...	,, ...	Sir Walter Scott
282	,, 11 ,, ...	,, ...	Coriolanus
283	,, 21 ,, ...	,, ...	Pygmalion
284	,, 31 ,, ...	,, ...	Galatea
285	Aug. 9 ,, ...	,, ...	Orpheus (No. 3)
286	,, 18 ,, ...	,, ...	Penelope
287	,, 27 ,, ...	,, ...	Ariadne
288	Sept. 5 ,, ...	,, ...	
	(Made for M. Lee)		
289	,, 13 ,, ...	Violin ...	
	(Made for Scott & Co.)		
290	,, 24 ,, ...	Violin ...	Elfin Shell
291	Oct. 3 ,, ...	,, ...	Eardale

No.	Date on which completed in the white.		Description.	Name.
292	Oct. 14, 1884	...	Violin	... A.E.I.
293	,, 26	,,	... Violoncello	... Sappho
294	Nov. 11	,,	... Viola	... Orpheus (No. 4)
295	,, 20	,,	... Violin	... Eurydice (No. 2)
296	,, 30	,,	... ,,	... The Elf
		(Made for Royal College)		
297	Dec. 20	,,	... Violoncello	... Apollo (No. 2)
		(Made for Scott & Co)		
298	,, 31	,,	... Violin	... Venetia
299	Jan. 12, 1885	... ,,		... Echo (No. 2)
300	Feb. 14	,, ... ,,		... No. 300
301	March 16	,, ... ,,		... Vestal
302	,, 31	,, ... ,,		... Mardale
303	April 15	,, ... ,,		... Venus of Milo
304	,, 22	,, ... ,,		... Abydos
305	,, 30	,, ... ,,		... Achilles
306	May 8	,, ... ,,		... Aeolus
307	,, 14	,, ... ,,		... Ancilla
308	,, 20	,, ... ,,		... Angelo
309	,, 30	,,	... Viola	... Anima
310	June 15	,,	... Violin	... Alesia
311	,, 26	,, ... ,,		... Stella
312	July 5	,, ... ,,		... Miranda
313	,, 15	,, ... ,,		... Victoria
314	,, 24	,, .. ,,		... Hero
315	Aug. 1	,,	. Violoncello	... Jupiter (No. 2)
		(for J. Homan, Esq.)		
316	,, 21	,,	... Violin	... Leander
317	,, 29	,, ... ,,		... Anacreon
318	Sept. 8	,, ... ,,		... Amber Witch

No.	Date on which completed in the white.			Description.		Name.
319	Sept.	16	,,	... Violin	...	Aristides
320	,,	26	,,	... ,,	...	Lord Byron
321	Oct.	7	,,	... ,,	...	Cambyses
322	,,	22	,,	... ,,	...	Cleopatra
323	,,	29	,,	... ,,	...	Cyrus
324	Nov.	10	,,	... ,,	...	Dido
325	,,	20	,,	... ,,	...	Rienzi
326	Dec.	7	,,	... ,,	...	Vasco da Gama
327	,,	19	,,	... ,,	...	Hannibal
328	,,	31	,,	... ,,	...	Corregio
329	Jan.	14, 1886	...	,,	...	Sueitielma
330	,,	23	,,	... ,,	...	Half Moon
331	Feb.	4	,,	... 'Cello Belly for Klotz		
332	,,	12	,,	... Violin	...	Miranda
333	,,	20	,,	... ,,	...	Murillo
334	March	4	,,	... Violoncello	...	Shelley
335	,,	18	,,	... Violin	...	Columbus
336	,,	30	,,	... ,,	...	Horace
337	April	7	,,	... Viola	...	Keats
338	,,	13	,,	... Violin	...	Milton
339	,,	24	,,	... ,,	...	Charlotte Brontë
340	May	1	,,	... ,,	...	Egmont
341	,,	10	,,	... ,,	...	Mignon
342	,,	17	,,	... ,,	...	Tennyson
343	,,	26	,,	... ,,	...	Wordsworth
344	June	4	,,	... ,,	...	Flora
345	,,	12	,,	... ,,	...	Loder
346	,,	21	,,	... ,,	...	Aurora

No.	Date on which completed in the white.		Description.	Name.
347	July	1, 1886	... Violin	... Una
348	,,	10 ,, ...	,,	... Vivaldi
349	,,	21 ,, ...	,,	... Sebastian Bach
350	Aug.	7 ,, ...	,,	... Bohemian
351	,,	17 ,, ...	,,	... Clytie
352	,,	28 ,, ...	,,	... Salisbury
353	Sept.	10 ,, ...	,,	... Beatrice de Fenda
354	,,	20 ,, ...	,,	... The Tone Poet
355	,,	30 ,, ...	,,	... Zephyr
356	Oct.	15 ,, ...	,,	... Pan
357	,,	27 ,, ...	,,	... Pythagoras
358	Nov.	3 ,,	New 'Cello Belly	
359	,,	10 ,, ...	Violin	... Egmont (No. 2)
360	,,	18 ,, ...	,,	... Calliope
361	,,	27 ,, ...	Violoncello...	Merlin
362	Dec.	15 ,, ...	Violin	... Bellona
363	,,	20 ,, ...	New Belly for Violin	
364	,,	28 ,, ...	Violin	... Cybelle
365	Jan.	7, 1887 ...	,,	... Iddlesleigh
366	,,	18 ,, ...	New Belly for "Preston"	
367	,,	24 ,, ...	Violin	... Idelia
368	Feb.	4 ,, ...	,,	... Proserpine
369	,,	14 ,, ...	,,	... Undine
370	March	10 ,, ...	,,	... Theseus
371	,,	21 ,, ...	,,	... Holbein
372	April	3 ,, ...	Viola	... Aned Reekie
373	,,	14 ,, ...	,,	... Antiope

No.	Date on which completed in the white.		Description.	Name.
374	April 27, 1887	...	Violin	... Orestes
375	May 8 ,,	...	,,	... Pylades
376	,, 12 ,,	...	Violoncello	... Eurycelus
377	,, 24 ,,	...	Violin	... Victoria Regina
378	June 8 ,,	...	,,	... Plutarch
379	,, 23 ,,	...	,,	... Nisus
380	July 8 ,,	...	,,	... Raphael
381	,, 23 ,,	... ·	,,	... Alexandra
382	Aug. 8 ,,	...	,,	... Bruce
383	,, 24 ,,	...	,,	... Rosalind
384	Sept. 6 ,,	...	,,	... Oceana
385	,, 21 ,,	...	Viola	... Rubens
386	Oct. 1 ,,	...	Violin	... Olitipa
387	,, 10 ,,	...	,,	... Clymene
388	,, 30 ,,	...	,,	... Agnes Sorel
389	Nov. 9 ,,	...	,,	... Iope
390	,, 18 ,,	...	,,	... Hippolyte
391	,, 30 ,,	...	,,	... Vulcan
392	Dec. 14 ,,	...	,,	... Diana
393	,, 27 ,,	...	,,	... Seneca
394	Jan. 5, 1888	...	,,	... Dante
395	,, 14 ,,	...	,,	... Aphrodyte
396	,, 26 ,,	...	,,	... Dr. Kane
397	Feb. 6 ,,	...	Violoncello	... Orestes
398	,, 28 ,,	...	Violin	... Apolonius
399	March 10 ,,	...	Viola	... Cyprian
400	April 10 ,,	...	Violin	... Apollo Belvedere
401	,, 26 ,,	...	,,	... Pelagia
402	May 5 ,,	...	,,	... Ulysses

No.	Date on which completed in the white.			Description.		Name,
403	May	15,	1888	...	Violin	... Daphne
404	,,	24	,,	...	,,	... Danæ
405	June	3	,,	...	,,	... Ustane
406	,,	14	,,	...	,,	... Isis
407	,,	25	,,	...	,,	... Chaucer
408	July	6	,,	...	,,	... Heliotrope
409	,,	19	,,	...	,,	... The Rose
410	,,	28	,,	...	,,	... Placidia
411	Aug.	10	,,	...	,,	... Arcadia
412	,,	31	,,	...	,,	... Pluto
413	Sept.	18	,,	...	,,	... Hypatia
414	,,	25	,,	...	,,	... Zenobra
415	Oct.	8	,,	...	,,	... Hesione
416	,,	15	,,	...	,,	... Orpheus (No. 5)
417	,,	21	,,	...	,,	... Luma
418	,,	29	,,	...	,,	... Canadian
419	Nov.	6	,,	...	,, ($\frac{3}{4}$ size)	Dido
420	,,	16	,,	...	,, .	... Arsenius
421	,,	26	,,	...	,,	... Vesta
422	Dec.	6	,,	...	,,	... Ovid
423	,,	13	,,	...	,,	... Aphleion
424	,,	21	,,	...	Viola	... Comet
425	,,	29	,,	...	Violin	... Hera
426	Jan.	9,	1889	...	,,	... Livingstone
427	,,	22	,,	...	,,	... Amabel
428	Feb.	7	,,	...	,,	... Asphodel
429	,,	18	,,	...	,, .	... Enid
430	March	5	,,	...	,,	... Lycurgus
431	,,	13	,,	...	,,	... Arcudin

No.	Date on which completed in the white.		Description.	Name.
432	March 28, 1889	...	Violin	... Alypsius
433	April 5	,, ...	,,	... Madame Patey
434	,, 16	,, ...	,,	... Cordelia (No. 1)
435	,, 26	,, ...	,,	... Orestes
436	May 1	,, ...	,,	... Messalina
437	,, 17	,, ...	,,	... Jenny Lind
438	,, 27	,, ...	,,	... C. Novello
439	June 5	,, ...	,,	... Ceylon Ruby
440	,, 22	,, ...	,,	... Pliny
441	,, 30	,, ...	,,	... Japonica
442	July 12	,, ...	,,	... Donizetti
443	,, 22	,, ...	,,	... Byron
444	,, 29	,, ...	,,	... Bottesini
445	Aug. 12	,, ...	,,	... Aeschylus
446	,, 20	,, ...	,,	... Christine Nilson
447	,, 28	,, ...	,,	... Calypso
448	Sapt. 19	,, ...	,,	... Nantilus
449	,, 19	,, ...	,,	... Tartene
450	,, 26	,, ...	,,	... Pygmalion
451	Oct. 11	,, ...	,,	... Prospero
452	,, 21	,, ...	,,	... Canova
453	Nov. 5	,, ...	,,	... Egonia
454	,, 14	,, ...	,,	... Isalim
455	,, 23	,, ...	,,	... Philarete
456	Dec. 5	,, ...	,,	...
457	,, 27	,, ...	,,	...
458	Jan. 4, 1890	...	,,	...
459	,, 10	,, ...	Viola	... Heloise
460	,, 18	,, ...	Violin	... Jupiter (No. 3)

No.	Date on which completed in the white.	Description.	Name.
461	Jan. 23, 1890	... Violin	... Praxitel
462	Feb. 1 ,,	... ,,	... Octavius
463	,, 8 ,,	... ,,	... Beatrice Cann
464	,, 18 ,,	... ,,	... Cymbeline
465	,, 26 ,,	... ,,	... Perugia
466	March 4 ,,	... ,,	... Guido
467	,, 13 ,,	... Viola	... Arsenius
468	,, 21 ,,	... Violin	... Chrisropher North
469	,, 27 ,,	... ,,	... Niobe
470	April 7 ,,	... ,,	... Ovid (No. 2)
471	., 15 ,,	... ,.	... Kreutzer
472	,, 19 ,,	... ,,	... Phidius
473	,, 62 ,,	... ,,	... Miranda
474	May 5 ,,	... ,, ($\frac{3}{4}$ size)	Billy
475	,, 12 ,,	... .,	... Cordova
476	,, 20 ,,	... ,,	... Horace (No. 2)
477	,, 26 ,,	... ,,	... Heliotrope (No. 2)
478	June 4 ,,	... ,,	... Venus di Medici
479	,, 11 ,,	... ,,	... Zelia
480	,, 19 ,,	... .,	... Miltiades
481	,, 28 ,,	... ,,	... Ethelrida
482	July 7 ,,	... ,,	... Sonambula
483	,, 14 ,,	... ,,	... Violet (No. 2)
484	,, 21 ,,	... ,,	... Gelsomina
485	.. 30 ,,	... ,,	... Neptune
486	Aug. 12 ,,	... ,,	... Neophyte
487	,, 21 ,.	... ,,	... Corelli
488	,, 26 ,,	... ,,	... Maritana
489	Sept. 2 ,,	... ,,	... Nero

No.	Date on which completed in the white.			Description.	Name.
490	Sept.	11, 1890	...	Viola	... Schiller
491	,,	22 ,,	...	Violin	... Tarisio
492	Oct.	2 ,,	...	,,	... Tartini
493	,,	11 ,,	...	,,	... Vulcan (No. 2)
494	,,	19 ,,	...	,,	... Rode
495	,,	29 ,,	...	,,	... Fisca
496	Nov.	5 ,,	...	Viola	... Molique
497	,,	13 ,,	...	Violin	... Ernst
498	,,	21 ,,	...	,,	... Kaliwoda
499	Dec.	4 ,,	...	Violoncello	... Zealand
500	,,	20 ,,	...	Violin	... No. 500
501	,,	27 ,,	...	,,	... Argos
502	,,	30 ,,	...	,,	... Antonina
503	Jan.	6, 1891	...	,,	... Astoria
504	,,	13 ,,	...	,,	... Arpani
505	,,	22 ,,	...	,,	... Pan (No. 2)
506	Feb.	3 ,,	...	,,	... Circe
507	,,	14 ,,	...	,,	... Lirden
508	,.	22 ,,	...	,,	... Aulis
509	March	7 ,,	...	,,	... Coria
510	,,	13 ,,	...	,,	... Ganymede
511	,,	23 ,,	...	,,	... Silonius
512	,,	30 ,,	...	,,	... Armivell
513	April	7 ,,	...	,,	... Camden
514	,,	12 ,,	...	,,	... Venus Victrix
515	,,	19 ,,	...	,,	... Julionus
516	,,	26 ,,	...	,,	... Three Fingers
517	May	5 ,,	...	,,	... Althæ
518	,,	14 ,,	...	,,	... Charlotte Corday

No.	Date on which completed in the white.			Description.	Name.
519	May	20,	1891 ...	Violin	... Pamela
520	,,	28	,, ...	,,	... Cynthia
521	June	5	,, ...	,,	... Eunice
522	,,	12	,, ...	,.	... Lincaster
523	July	8	,, ...	,,	... Ivanhoe
524	,,	15	,, ...	,,	... Juno (No. 2)
525	,,	22	,, ...	,,	... Adelon
526	,,	29	,, ...	,,	... Pope
527	Aug.	7	,, ...	,,	... Leonidas
528	,,	14	,, ...	,,	... Rydal
529	,,	22	,, ...	,,	... Celia
530	Sept.	1	,, ...	,,	... Dunmail
531	,,	9	,, ...	,,	... Cressida
532	,,	16	,, ...	,,	... Astrolabe
533	,,	23	,, ...	,,	... Troilus
534	Oct.	2	,, ...	,,	... Soracte
535	,,	13	,, ...	,,	... Isidorus
536	,,	23	,, ...	,,	... Calydon
537	Nov.	2	,, ...	,,	... Ceres
538	,,	11	,, ...	,,	... Gœthe
539	,,	23	,, ...	,,	... Minerva
540	Dec.	5	,, ...	,,	... Mozart
541	,,	12	,, ...	,,	... Eunice (No. 2)
542	,,	21	,, ...	,,	... Rasselas
543	,,	30	,, ...	,,	... Rembrandt
544	Jan.	6,	1892 ...	,,	... Josephine
545	,,	14	,, ...	,,	... Prometheus (No. 2)
546	,,	23	,, ...	,,	... Morrielle
547	,,	30	,, ...	,,	... Petrarch

No.	Date on which completed in the white.			Description.	Name.
548	Feb.	7,	1892	... Violin	... Albert Victor
549	,,	16	,,	... Viola	... Robert Bruce
550	,,	23	,,	... Violin	... Diana (No. 2)
551	,,	29	,,	... ,,	... Cleopatra (No. 2)
552	March	10	,,	... ,,	... Albert Victor (No. 2)
553	,,	27	,,	.. ,,	.. Estelle
554	,,	31	,,	.. ,,	.. Egerice
555	April	8	,,	.. ,,	.. Plutus
556	,,	29	,,	.. ,,	.. Alaric
557	May	8	,,	.. ,,	.. Monica
558	,,	19	,,	.. ,,	.. Titania
559	,,	28	,,	.. ,,	.. Algœ
560	June	6	,,	.. ,,	.. Bianca D'Oria
561	,,	14	,,	.. ,,	.. Una (No. 2)
562	,,	23	,,	.. ,,	.. Calypso
563	July	2	,,	.. ,,	.. Hector
564	,,	15	,,	.. ,,	.. Constance
565	,,	21	,,	.. ,,	.. Viviette
566	Aug.	1	,,	.. ,,	.. Rowena
567	,,	9	,,	.. ,,	.. Alexa
568	,,	18	,,	.. ,,	.. The Druid
569	Sept.	13	,,	.. ,,	.. Circe (No. 2)
570	,,	21	,,	.. ,,	.. Tennyson (In Memoriam)
571	Oct.	9	,,	.. ,,	.. Sardonapolis
572	,,	17	,,	.. ,,	.. Derwent
573	,,	28	,,	.. ,,	.. Julius Cæsar
574	Nov.	8	,,	.. ,,	.. Jupiter Strator
575	,,	17	,,	.. ,,	.. The Zebra

No.	Date on which completed in the white.		Description.		Name.
576	Nov. 27, 1892	..	Violin	..	Cordelia (No. 2)
577	Dec. 7 ,,	..	,,	..	The Monarch (No. 2)
578	,, 19 ,,	..	,,	..	Antinous
579	Jan. 3, 1893	..	Violoncello	..	Harold
580	,, 30 ,,	..	Viola	..	Helena Forman
581	Feb. 11 ,,	..	Violin	..	Reubens (No. 2)
582	,, 22 ,,	..	,, (carved back)	..	Old Windsor
583	March 14 ,,	..	,,	..	Hecuba
584	,, 22 ,,	..	,,	..	Mars
585	April 15 ,,	..	,, (carved back)	..	Convolvulus
586	,, 25 ,,	..	,,	..	Midas
587	May 6 ,,	..	,,	..	Sirus
588	,, 15 ,,	..	,,	..	Odinatus
589	,, 25 ,,	..	,,	..	Arcturus
590	June 2 ,,	..	,,	..	Palladus
591	,, 9 ,,	..	,,	..	The Titan
592	,, 19 ,,	..	,,	..	Polaris
593	,, 23 ,,	..	,,	..	Agricola
594	July 8 ,,	..	,,	..	Capella
595	,, 18 ,,	..	,,	..	Marcagni
596	,, 28 ,,	..	,,	..	Veronica
597	Aug. 6 ,,	..	,,	..	The Cardinal
598	,, 18 ,,	..	,,	..	Hengist
599	,, 28 ,,	..	,,	..	Horsa
600	Sept. 6 ,,	..	,,	..	Tithonus
601	,, 15 ,,	..	,,	..	Eros
602	,, 22 ,,	..	,,	..	Violante

No.	Date on which completed in the white.	Description.	Name.
603	Oct. 3, 1893	.. Violin	.. Neptune (No. 2)
604	„ 10 „ .. „		.. Lærtes
605	„ 20 „ .·. „		.·. Ithaca
606	Nov. 1 „ .. „		.·. Estelle (No. 2)
607	„ 10 „ .·. „		.. Haydn
608	„ 20 „ .. „		.. Mozart
609	Dec. 9 „ .. Viola		.·. Schubert
610	„ 24 „ .·. Violoncello..		Beethoven

Second Series.

This Quartette was made for
Gustav Sandberg, of Göteborg, Sweden.

No.	Date	Description.	Name.
611	Jan. 15, 1894	.. Violin	.. De Medici
612	„ 25 „ .. „		.. Archytus
613	Feb. 4 „ .. „		.. Antigoni
614	„ 12 „ .. „		.. Aurora
615	„ 22 „ ..· „		.. Adéle
616	March 7 „ .·. „		.. Orlando di Lasse
617	„ 18 „ .. „		.. Botticelli
618	„ 31 „ .. „		.. Idalia
619	April 10 „ .. „		.. Cato
620	„ 18 „ .. „		.. Pylos
621	May 5 „ .·. „		.. Atys
622	„ 16 „ .·. „		.. Spirit of the Dawn
623	„ 29 „ .. „		.·. Palestrina
624	June 8 „ .·. „		.. Phryne
625	„ 29 „ .. „		.. Atalanta
626	July 11 „ .·. „		.. King Arthur
627	„ 25 „ .. „		.. Eudocia
628	Aug. 3 „ .. „		.. Leontius
629	„ 11 „ .·. „		.. Athenais

No.	Date on which completed in the white.		Description.	Name.
630	Aug. 24, 1894	..	Violin	.. Placidia (No. 2)
631	Sept. 3	,, ..	,,	.. Sarah Bernhardt
632	,, 11	,, ..	,,	.. Othyssius
633	,, 22	,, ..	,,	.. Eurotas
634	Oct. 3	,, ..	,,	.. Ina
635	,, 12	,, ..	,,	.. Ilcatello
636	,, 22	,, ..	,,	.. Euryanthe
637	Nov. 6	,, ..	,,	.. Evelyn
638	,, 21	,, ..	,,	.. Menelaus
639	Dec. 3	,, ..	,,	.. Caliphronas
640	,, 13	,, ..	,,	.. Nestor
641	,, 24	,, ..	,,	.. Hispania
642	Jan. 7, 1895	..	,,	.. Daphne
643	,, 23	,, ..	,,	.. Euryalus
644	Feb. 1	,, ..	,,	.. Aure
645	,, 12	,, ..	,,	.. Venus Urania
646	,, 22	,, ..	,,	.. La Tosca
647	March 8	,, ..	,,	.. Theodora
648	,, 18	,, ..	,,	.. Mercury
649	,, 30	,, ..	,,	.. Somell
650	April 10	,, ..	,,	.. Isopel
651	,, 20	,, ..	,,	.. Fedora
652	May 4	,, ..	,,	.. Cynesia
653	,, 16	,, ..	,,	.. St. Kentigern
654	,, 28	,, ..	,,	.. Euclid
655	June 10	,, ..	,,	.. Belle Isle
656	,, 21	,, ..	,,	.. Ermerilda
657	July 4	,, ..	,,	.. Elinor

No.	Date on which completed in the white.	Description.	Name.
658	July 16, 1895	Violin	Omphall
659	„ 31 „	„	Daffodil
660	Aug. 12 „	„	Carlo Crovelli
661	„ 26 „	„	Celeste
662	Sept. 7 „	„	Magnum Bonam
663	Oct. 9 „	„	The Check
664	„ 20 „	„	Felicia
665	„ 30 „	„	Rose of Allandale
666	Nov. 10 „	„	Sappho (No. 2)
667	„ 25 „	„	Pharan
668	Dec. 3 „	„	Cytherea
669	„ 16 „	„	Palladas (No. 2)
670	„ 25 „	„	Hallè
671	Jan. 12, 1896	„	Lampeto
672	„ 25 „	„	Ariosto
673	Feb. 6 „	„	Cassius
674	„ 20 „	„	Fiordelisa
675	„ 29 „	„	Azræl
676	March 16 „	„	Genevra
677	„ 27 „	„	Princess
678	April 12 „	„	Aufugus
679	„ 23 „	„	Florinel
680	May 4 „	„	Elusidis
681	„ 14 „	„	Epictetus
682	„ 24 „	„	Hermione
683	June 9 „	„	Mæcenas
684	„ 23 „	„	Catullus
685	July 8 „	„	Antiope

No.	Date on which completed in the white.			Description.		Name.
686	July	19,	1896 ..	Violin	.,	Coralie
687	„	31	„ . ,	„	.,	Lesbia
688	Aug.	12	„ . ,	„	.,	Abidos
689	„	20	„ . ,	„	,,	Anderida
690	Sept.	3	„ . .,	„	.,	Thalestris
691	„	16	„ . .	„	.	Ephyre
692	Oct.	22	„ . ,	„	.,	Spirit of Song
693	Nov.	11	„ . .	„	..,	Juna Moneta
694	„	24	„ . .	„	..,	Othone
695	Dec.	5	„ . ,	„	.,	Blanche
696	„	24	„ ..	„	..	Soutag
697	Jan.	10,	1897 ..	„	..	Cimarosa
698	„	25	„ ..,	„	..,	Kreutzer (No. 2)
699	Feb.	5	„ ..	„	..,	Thalberg
700	„	28	„ ...	„	..,	Jubilee
701	March	18	„ . ,	„	.,	Auber
702	„	25	„	{ Two Violins made for Jacob Lomax, Bolton. }		No name or label
703	April	6	„			
704	„	14	„	.. Violin	..	Robert Burns
705	„	27	„	.., „	...	Caledon
706	May	11	„	.. „	...	Sterndale Bennett
707	„	26	„	., „	.:	Isidor
708	June	15	„	., „	..	Palestrina (No. 2)
709	July	17	„	., „	.:	Mariana
710	Aug.	7	„	.., „	..,	Farinelli
711	„	25	„	.. „	..	The Feather
712	Sept.	20	„	.. „	.,	Auboyne
713	Oct.	17	„	.., „	..,	Vestris

No.	Date on which completed in the white.	Description.	Name.
714	Jan. 3, 1898 ..	Violin	.. Aenone
715	Feb. 10 „ ..	„	.. Prudent
716	March 1 „ ..	„	.. Leila
717	„ 28 „ ..	„	.. Violet (No. 3)
718	April 9 „ ..	„	.. Neil Gow
719	„ 20 „ ..	„	.. The Nightingale
720	May 5 „ ..	„	.. Celeste (No. 2)
721	„ 19 „ ..	„	.. W. E. Gladstone
722	June 1 „ ..	„	.. Aeolus
723	„ 17 „ ..	„	.. Coronis
724	„ 29 „ ..	„	.. Flotow
725	July 13 „ ..	„	.. St. George
726	„ 25 „ ..	„	.. Tisiphone
727	Aug. 11 „ ..	„	.. John Ruskin
728	„ 28 „ ..	„	.. Caligula
729	Sept. 20 „ ..	„	.. Bonnie Dundee
730	Oct. 1 „ ..	„	.. The Snake
731	„ 16 „ ..	„ (carved back)..	Thirlmere
732	Nov. 8 „ ..	„ „ ..	Blea Tarn
733	Dec. 3 „ ..	Viola „ ..	Westdale
734	„ 20 „ ..	Violin	.. Myvanwy
735	Jan. 23, 1899 ..	„	.. Avonia
736	March 20 „ ..	„	.. Amber Witch (No.2)
737	April 5 „ ..	„	.. Ostera
738	„ 19 „ ..	„	.. Virgilia
739	May 12 „ ..	„	.. Lucian
740	„ 28 „ ..	„	.. Aspirante
741	June 16 „ ..	„	.. Hazilia

No.	Date on which completed in the white.	Description.	Name.
742	July 7, 1899 ..	Violin	.. Pentelicus
743	Aug. 7 ,, ..	,,	.. The London
	(First made in London)		
744	Sept. 8 ,, ..	Violin	.. Salsette
745	,, 28 ,, ..	,,	.. Elephanta
746	Oct. 14 ,, ..	,,	.. The Opal
747	Nov. 4 ,, ..	,,	.. Harry Lavender
748	Jan. 1, 1900 ..	,,	.. A Challenge to Cremona
749	Feb. 10 ,, ..	,,	.. Israfel
750	March 23 ,, ..	,,	.. Lord Roberts
751	April 15 ,, ..	,,	.. Sir Redvers Buller
752	May 9 ,, ..	,,	.. Jason
753	,, 30 ,, ..	,,	.. Mafeking
754	June 15 ,, ..	,,	.. General French
755	,, 30 ,, ..	,,	.. Sir Claude McDonald
756	July 20 ,, ..	,,	.. Baden Powell
757	,, 30 ,, ..	,,	.. Merlin
758	Aug. 25 ,, ..	,,	.. Nivienne
759	Sept. 23 ,, ..	,,	.. Queen of the Air
760	Oct. 20 ,, ..	,,	.. The Dragon
761	Nov. 9 ,, ..	,,	.. Aeonian
762	,, 28 ,, ..	,,	.. Strathcona
763	Dec. 20 ,, ..	,,	.. Vestris (No. 2)
764	Jan. 15, 1901 ..	,,	.. Half Moon (No. 2)
765	,, 25 ,, ..	,,	.. Messalina
766	Feb. 10 ,, ..	Violoncello..	King Edward VII
767	April 27 ,, ..	Violin	.. Nuogen
768	May 10 ,, ..	,,	.. Sir A. Milner

No.	Date on which completed in the white.	Description.	Name.
769	May 26, 1901	.. Violin	.. Dion Cassino
770	June 11 ,,	.. ,,	.. Belinda
771	,, 22 ,,	.. ,,	.. Honoria
772	July 13 ,,	.. Viola	.. Mainteuon
773	Aug. 4 ,,	.. Violin	.. Kitchener
774	,, 20 ,,	.. ,,	.. Elgiva
775	Sept. 4 ,,	.. ,,	.. Alfred the Great
776	,, 20 ,,	.. ,,	.. Alexandrina
777	Oct. 6 ,,	.. ,,	.. Queen Alexandra
778	,, 26 ,,	.. ,,	.. Mitylene
779	Nov. 11 ,,	.. ,,	.. Addison
780	Dec. 1 ,,	.. ,, (carved back)	Ivy
781	,, 30 ,,	.. ,,	.. Cœur de Lion
782	Jan. 15, 1902 ..	,, (carved back)	Eveline
783	,, 30 ,,	.. ,,	.. Adalina
784	March 20 ,,	.. ,,	.. Cecil Rhodes
785	April 10 ,,	.. ,,	.. Drusilla
786	,, 25 ,,	.. ,,	.. Persephone
787	May 9 ,,	.. ,, (carved back)	Anemone (No. 3)
788	,, 25 ,,	.. ,,	.. Pretorius
789	June 10 ,,	.. ,,	.. Yolande
790	,, 26 ,,	.. ,, (carved back)	Coronation Edward VII
791	Aug. 10 ,,	.. ,,	.. Ethelberta
792	Sept. 10 ,,	.. ,,	.. Margaret of Anjou
793	,, 20 ,,	.. ,, (carved back)	Water Lily

No.	Date on which completed in the white.	Description.	Name.
794	Oct. 12, 1902	.. Violin	.. Leila (No. 2)
795	,, 25 ,,	.. ,,	.. Elma
796	Nov. 20 ,,	.. ,,	.. Clarise
797	Dec. 10 ,,	.. ,,	.. Althæ
798	Jan. 7, 1903	.. ,,	.. J. Chamberlain
799	Feb. 4 ,,	.. Viola	.. Berlioz
800	March 9 ,,	.. Violin	.. No. 800
801	April 4 ,,	.. ,,	.. Asphodel (No. 2)
802	,, 20 ,,	.. ,,	.. Great Heart
803	May 16 ,,	.. ,,	.. Panope
804	June 17 ,,	.. Viola	.. Iphigenia
805	July 10 ,,	.. Violin	.. Rosamond
806	Aug. 12 ,,	.. ,,	.. Meredith Morris
807	Sept. 20 ,,	.. ,,	.. The Pearl
808	Oct. 20 ,,	.. ,,	.. Cedric
809	Nov. 27 ,,	.. ,,	.. The Moonstone
810	Dec. 16 ,,	.. ,,	.. Idylle

(Made for Sir Wm. Ingram, Bart.)

| 811 | 1904 | .. Back & Belly |

(The instrument was completed by R. A. Stanley).

Appendix B.

The Mayson Family Register.

Walter Henry Mayson, youngest son of Mark Mayson, of Portinscale, Keswick, was married to (1) Katharine Mary Elwood, eldest daughter of Mr. Elwood, of Winton, near Manchester, on the 24th of December, 1863.

(Katharine May Mayson died in 1864).

(2) Elizabeth King, widow of Frank King, on June 20th, 1866, by whom he had issue as follows:

(1) *Sarah Elizabeth,* born at 1 Chapel Lane, Cheetham Hill, Manchester, on April 7th, 1867.

(2) *Walter Henry,* born at Hill View, Cheetham Hill, on March 23rd, 1869. Died July, 1906.

(3) *Stansfield*, born at Hill View, Cheetham Hill, on October 2nd, 1870.

(4) *Florence Gertrude*, born at The Polygon, Lower Broughton, November 2nd, 1874.

(5) *Ida*, born at Somerville Cottage, Prestwick, on October 8th, 1878. Died in the same year.

(6) *Leonora Beatrice*, born at Hayden Terrace, Crumpsall, Manchester, on June 30th, 1880.

London
Nov 8/99

My dear Mr. Morris

I ought to have written
you y. day, but have jotted
down a few names, of which
you make safe use.
None (or only one or two)
are of the upper crust.

I sent on Label as requested;
and I enclose 2 rubbed JS
holes for your guidance.
One is off the extreme on those
of what is except as Elephants;
the other where edge is turned.

your work of love — all my life has been one of struggles with adversity and narrow minded prejudice. But I am certain where true genius is, there, also, will be stumbling blocks; and that the Giver of the talent gives also His strength — for such I have never lacked.

The high compliment you pay me as to being the modern Stradivari has been frequently paid me before, but is most welcome from you.

I hope you will now find all in order; if not write again to

Yours Sincerely
Walter H. Mayson

FACSIMILE OF LABELS.

Walter H. Mayson,
Manchester, Fecit.
vsv. " Isidor "   1897.

Deus adsit, obsit Mundus.

WALTER H. MAYSON,
MANCHESTER.

No.   A.D.

CPSIA information can be obtained
at www.ICGtesting.com
Printed in the USA
BVHW051651260623
666400BV00007B/385